A Hood C

MW01591088

A

Hood Chick's

Story

Part II

Presented by

LaShonda DeVaughn

LaShonda DeVaughn

Editor: www.hightowereditorialservices.com

In Loving Memory of

Andre Stone….

We did it again lil bro!

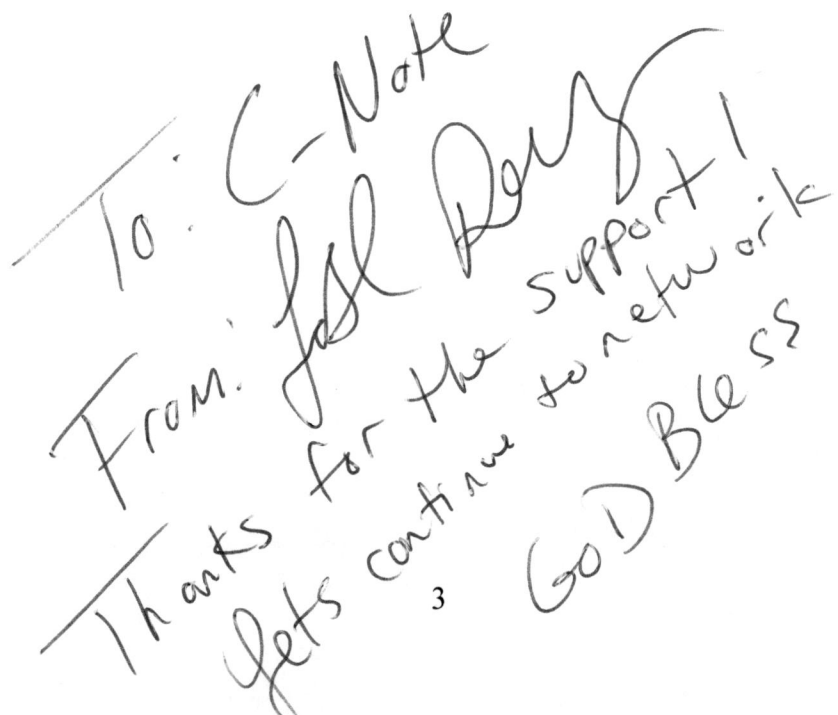

To: C-Note

From: [signature]

Thanks for the support!

lets continue to network

GOD Bless

LaShonda DeVaughn

A Hood Chick's Story Part 2

I told y'all I wouldn't give up....

-FIVE YEARS LATER-

Chapter One- *My new life with Tony*

"Thank you Jesus!" I said to myself while staring at the chocolate treat that I had the pleasure of melting in last night. I was laying in the bed of our fresh juices after three rounds of pleasurable sex. Tony's sexy ass was getting dressed in front of the bureau. It was Friday afternoon and we'd taken a half day off work to get an early start on our weekend.

He slid on his fresh True Religion jeans, Timberland boots and a crisp white Tee. On weekdays he would rock Versace or Hugo Boss suits because of his business. I had the best of both worlds; I was engaged to a corporate thug. When Tony was released from prison, he went back in the game and eventually used all of his drug money and turned it

A Hood Chick's Story Part II

legal. He opened up a mortgage company in the heart of downtown Boston and it's been successful for two years. He also cut his braids when he got out and was now rocking a low cut fade. His cut definitely gave him more of a professional look, but he was still my sexy thug.

His clothes were now neatly assembled on his body and he brushed his hand over his waves checking himself out in the mirror.

"You know you look good," I said from the bed. He turned around examining my nude caramel body lying gracefully in the bed.

"Nah *you* look good," he said walking toward me before bending down on his knees. He spread my legs apart and stuck his tongue into my kitty and started using the skills that forced me to release seductive moans.

Our sex life was the bomb, he loved French kissing the cat and I loved pleasing him.

I took my hands cuffing the back of his head and turned it round and round while spreading my legs further and further apart. Tony willingly dug his head further into my kitty defining the true meaning of "giving some head".

After making sure that I was satisfied by sucking on my clit until my orgasm forced me to scoot away from his mouth, he looked me in the eyes and smiled. I was turned on by the juices that I left around his mouth because I knew that he loved making me feel good.

LaShonda DeVaughn

He went into the bathroom to wash his face and brush his teeth while I lay lazily in bed recovering from yet another orgasm. My body was so relaxed and drained from all of the love making that I just laid there smiling in bliss. There was never a dull moment with us. Tony basically taught me everything I knew about sex and turned me into his true to the heart freak.

"Come on Tiara, you gotta get up and get dressed!" he yelled out from the bathroom inside of our bedroom. I tried to pull myself out of bed but I was exhausted. As soon as I sat up, I laid back down to try to snatch up a few more seconds of rest.

Tony and I were supposed to pick up our daughter from my friend Renee's house and then head to New York. We planned to shop for clothes, shoes and jewelry, something we did quite often. Tony was spontaneous like that; he kept the spark flaming in our relationship. He always told me that there wasn't anything that he wouldn't do for me and my daughter. He spoiled us rotten, we didn't want for nothing and he referenced us as his girls who he would go to the end of the world for. Plus the fact that he had been locked up the first three years of our daughter's life made him go even harder at making up for lost time.

It had been two years since he'd been out of jail from doing a three year bid. When he was released from prison, he had to do something quick to move my daughter

6

and me out of the projects and into something more livable. He went right back to hustling and I mean hustling *hard*. Weed, coke, crack, the works. And before we knew it, he had enough money to buy us our own home.

He copped us a beautiful five bedroom house in Avon that was built the same year we purchased it. It was about fifteen to twenty minutes away from the hood in a beautiful suburban neighborhood surrounded by mostly trees. It was a dramatic change for me after living in the projects with Renee for three years. But it was perfect enough for me to begin my new life with my family putting all the bullshit that almost made me give up on everything and everybody in the past.

My new life gave me hope and I was finally happy again for the first time in a long time. I felt free and when I dwelled on my past, I blocked it out by putting more energy and focus into Tony and my daughter; they were truly all that I had in my life that was constant. I couldn't complain about my new living situation either. Our new home had beautiful gleaming hardwood flooring throughout, marble in the kitchen with peppered gray and black granite countertops and stainless steel appliances; the shit was off the chain. The living room boasted large bay windows that let in a great portion of sunlight during the day, old fashioned style moldings and recessed lights that beamed from the high ceilings. I made sure that I hooked it up so that it looked like it had just graced a page of an IKEA magazine. Tony spent a fortune on our home but it was definitely worth it. And he didn't stop at our home. He knew that since we had a child that he couldn't keep hustling as his full time gig. So we did a great deal of research and commercial property searching until we found the perfect spot and that's when he opened up the mortgage company.

I was now able to put my community college degree to work by managing the office and overseeing all of the employees. I always joked with Tony telling him that our life was like that Mary J. Blige song because I was his *lover* and his *secretary*.

I finally managed to get my lazy ass out of bed and got dressed. I met Tony outside where he was waiting impatiently in his big body 745 Beamer. He loved that damn car. My body was still weak and it showed in my walk because I was dragging my feet. Tony was inside the car bobbing his head to his DJ Drama mixed CD that he had turned up loud enough for the neighbors to dance to. He turned to look at me through his dark tinted D&G sunglasses. "T, why you walking so slow? We have to hurry up and get to the hood to get the baby and then be out, I don't wanna hit traffic."

"Okay baby I'm coming," I said moving just a step faster before approaching the passenger side of the car.

A Hood Chick's Story Part II

We referred to our daughter Shayonna as "the baby" but she was actually five years old. She's the cutest thing that sight has ever laid eyes on. She has a beautiful butter cream complexion, long hair that I often kept braided with beads hanging from them and chinky eyes that looked like she had on permanent eyeliner. She's a daddy's girl but she loves me all the same. Every time I looked in her eyes I saw my little brother who was killed five years ago when I was pregnant with her but it still seems like yesterday.

I opened the car door and plopped inside the passenger seat and we were finally off to pick up the baby.

At each red light Tony would put his right hand in between my legs and softly rub my kitty.

"Lean back," he said.

I sucked in my bottom lip and pushed the automatic clutch to lay my seat back and Tony drove away. He drove while putting one hand down my panties fingering me in slow circular intervals and the other on the steering wheel. We did freaky shit like this all the time; we couldn't get enough of each other. He continued fingering my clit faster until I climaxed. I slouched comfortably in the passenger seat with my eyes closed enjoying the intense ecstasy that he took me to for the fifth time today.

Tony tried to unbuckle his pants while he drove, he looked over at me licking his juicy ass lips giving me that sexy gangsta look and I knew that he wanted some head. He

LaShonda DeVaughn

pulled out his chocolate stick and stroked it while I pressed the clutch to pull my seat back up. Just as I was crawling over with one hand on Tony's lap he shouted, "Damn!"

I looked up at him; I thought something severe had happened, "What's the matter baby?" I asked.

He sucked his teeth. "Man, we are here already!" he pouted. I sat up to look out the window and I saw the projects that I stayed at with Renee during the entire time Tony was locked up.

"Baby can you just suck it a little in the parking lot?"

I gave Tony "the look."

"Hell no Tony! I used to be one of them nosy chicks looking out of the window into people's cars when I lived here. We just have to wait till we get to the hotel in New York. Don't worry about it baby, you know I'm gonna hook you up."

Tony looked at me, his hand was still on his dick. I frowned my face pretending to sympathize with him. "I'm sorry baby, I got you in N-Y trust me." I opened the door and looked back at him.

"I'm about to go get the baby, I'll be right back."

On my way to the door I saw a few people that I knew, they waved at me or nodded their heads to acknowledge me. This girl Bianca who used to babysit my

10

A Hood Chick's Story Part II

daughter when I would visit Tony when he was locked up ran over to me. "Hey Tiara."

"What's up?" I replied.

She looked me up and down checking out my gear.

Now that I was back on my feet, I was always rocking some fly shit and Bianca always noticed. Bianca was a cool chick, if she wasn't, I damn sure wouldn't have let her be around my daughter, but she was a good girl. She was a freshman in College and I knew that she had a good head on her shoulders.

"We miss your around here." She said.

I sucked my teeth. "Girl please! I couldn't stay here any longer especially with Shayonna."

"I feel you" she said.

"Did you get to see her yet?" I asked.

"Yeah I was up in Renee's crib earlier today playing with her, she's getting so big and more beautiful than ever."

I smiled, "Thank you, she get it from her Mama."

We both laughed.

Bianca checked out my gear again and stopped at my shoes, "Your shoes are fire girl, where you get them from?" she asked.

"I got them from Jimmy Choo in Copley."

"Those are hot!"

"Thanks, but let me go in here to get my baby, you take care 'kay'?" I said finally cutting her short.

11

LaShonda DeVaughn

"A'ight you too."

As Bianca walked away I saw her looking hard in Tony's car. I was looking back the entire time to see why the hell she was staring at him so hard. She was a cool chick but she knew the deal with me, she know I don't play that shit. She finally turned in another direction and kept it moving. I guess you could say I was overreacting. Tony really never gave me any reason not to trust him so I didn't know why I would often trip. I guess I just knew how some gold digging hoes were, especially chicks who didn't care if they were breaking up a happy home. So I didn't trust no one because I would break a bitch's neck *and* his.

The only time that I doubted Tony's trust was before he got locked up. I had just moved in with him and my ex friend Ke-Ke and I were headed inside his crib when we spotted some smut that he fucked from back in the day popping up at the crib. Ke-Ke and I whooped her ass so bad that she became the reason that Tony got locked up. The bitch went to the police and snitched on him telling them who he was, what he was selling and where he lived. He had to do three years over that ho. Messing with smuts will do that to you. That's why niggas need to start using their dick radar a little better or better yet being faithful to their girls.

Till this day, I don't know her reason for popping up at Tony's house back then. I don't know if she came to fuck or if he was even cheating on me or not but all I did know

12

was that the broad thought she got her ass whooped then, if I had ever saw her again, I'd probably kill her.

I had to live in the projects for three years on welfare struggling to raise my daughter while living in Renee's living room with a million of her siblings barely getting by. When I say that I struggled for the three years Tony was locked up, I STRUGGLED, there is no denying that. I had to keep washing the same five or six outfits for my daughter and me to get by. Shit was hard and I thought about that girl every time I felt a tear glaze my eye for the way that I was living. The bitch made a wise move though, I heard she moved to one of the islands, she was Haitian or Jamaican or something so she fled with her family in fear of Tony finding her. I walked through the piss smelling project hall that I didn't miss one bit and arrived at Renee's door and gave three strong knocks.

"Who is it?" I heard a young sweet familiar voice sang out and I smiled.

"It's Mommy." My baby girl opened the door, her eyes lit up when she saw me.

"Mommee," she chimed out before diving into my arms. I picked her and all of her five year old weight up like she was a toddler. I had missed her so much. It was hard going just one day without seeing her.

"Hey Sweety, did you miss me?" I asked.

"Yes I did Mommy, where's Daddy?"

I playfully rolled my eyes, "Where's daddy? What about Mommy? I missed you too."

"Mommy, I missed both of y'all."

I placed her back on the floor and called out for Renee.

"Renee!" My voice echoed but no one answered back.

I looked down at my daughter.

"Baby, where is Renee?"

She batted her eyes and pointed to Renee's bedroom door like she was grown and shook her head and said, "She's probably in there on the phone as usual."

I knocked on Renee's door once, and then let myself in. I was shocked at what I saw. This bitch had the nerve to be on the bed fuckin' some nigga. The sound of the door opening startled them and I could tell that they thought I was my daughter coming in because they tried to cover up quick.

"Oh shit!" Renee screamed out.

The funny looking dude she was fuckin' looked up at me and then began pulling the covers over his face. I stepped out of the room which smelled like dead fish and ass and began rushing my daughter to the front door. Renee pulled one of the sheets off of her bed and stormed behind me trying to explain herself.

"My fault T, I didn't know you would be here that quick."

A Hood Chick's Story Part II

I turned around and shut my eyes for a second before I spoke to gather my thoughts.

"Renee, what if I was Shayonna coming in that room?" Renee glanced over at the wall to avoid looking me in the eyes.

"Your ass still haven't changed Renee, that shit ain't cute."

Renee was my homey and I loved her to death, but she was always with a different dude. Even when we were younger she was still exactly how she was now, it was so sad to see that she hadn't changed any of her chickenhead ways. The niggas she would fuck could give a fuck about her, she would fuck them just to get what she could, twenty or fifty dollars here and there and then brag like the nigga was taking care of her. She didn't care if he had a girl or not, as long as she was getting something out of it, she was straight scandalous but I still loved her trifling ass like a sister.

"Well, I don't know if my baby will be coming back over here, she don't need to be around none of that," I said pointing toward her room where that scrub lay waiting for her in her bed. I was so frustrated looking at my homegirl, she was so pretty but made all the wrong choices. And frankly she was too old to still be sleeping around, we weren't little teenagers anymore, it was time to settle down.

"Damn! You could have at least waited until I picked her up." I shook my head and continued. "Nah Renee man, I can't have her over here around you and your men." I covered my daughter's ears. "The dick couldn't have been that good."

Renee sucked her teeth. "Come on T, don't do that, she's my little boo too." She shifted the sheet around her body and covered herself as best as she could and squat to talk to Shayonna.

"Didn't we have fun Shay?"

My daughter's innocent smile lit up and she replied, "Yeah."

"That's my girl, give Auntie Renee a kiss."

Shayonna planted a kiss on Renee's cheek and Renee stood up still looking down at Shayonna, "I'll see you soon okay?"

"Okay." Shayonna replied and we began stepping out of Renee's apartment into the hallway.

"T?" Renee stopped me when I was halfway down the hall and I turned around.

"I said I'm sorry a'ight?"

I cracked a smile, "You know you were wrong for that right?

"I know T, my fault, it won't happen again okay?"

"A'ight, get your nasty ass back in the house."

Renee smiled and tip toed back into her crib.

A Hood Chick's Story Part II

"Dadeeeee!!!" My daughter sang out as we exited the building. Tony was standing outside of the car ready to greet her.

"How's daddy's baby?"

"I'm good daddy, can we go get some ice cream at Regal's?"

"Sure, anything for my baby girl."

I paused and gave Tony a two second stare, "Baby, you know we don't have time to stop at Regal's to get ice cream."

"If my baby girl want ice cream, that's what she's getting." He said sternly.

"Yessss!" Shayonna happily blurted out as she hopped into the backseat.

There was never talking Tony out of anything when it came to Shayonna, that's why she adored him so much. He could never say no to her.

We ended up spending a half an hour at Regal's slurping down ice cream and spending quality family time together. And just like I had predicted, we hit hella traffic. The four hour drive to New York from Boston turned into six. Shayonna and I slept most of the way, every time I opened my eyes to see how far we had gotten, we were still bumper to bumper with other cars. I knew that this meant that we had to shop early Saturday morning because most of the stores that we normally shopped at would be closed when we got there.

Overly exhausted, we arrived in New York and we checked in to the Marriott. We got a beautiful two bedroom suite so that the baby could have her own room and her daddy and I could have our privacy.

"Y'all hungry?" Tony asked.

"Yeah baby I'm starving."

"I'm hungry too daddy." Shayonna said bouncing up and down on me and Tony's king size bed as if she didn't just wake up from a nap in the car. I sat on the edge of the bed and flipped off my shoes as my mouth watered thinking about the food that I wanted.

"Baby, get me some greens, chitterlings, yams and macaroni and cheese."

Tony smirked as if I just wasted my breath. "Baby, you know I already know what you want."

He bent over and gave me a soft peck on the lips and left.

Tony and I completed each other, if we went to Mickey D's, Wendy's or a local sub shop, we knew just what to get each other. We were on point with each other like that.

While he was out picking up our food, I made sure that I bathed Shayonna, combed her hair and put on her night

A Hood Chick's Story Part II

clothes so that she was comfortable enough to jump right in bed after we ate because I wanted some QT with her father.

When Tony returned with our favorite soul food from Sylvia's, we grubbed on it like it was Thanksgiving dinner. Our New York trips just wouldn't be complete if we didn't get any Sylvia's, it was famous for its divine soul food and I knew why, the food was the shit and we dogged it until our bellies were full.

I tucked Shayonna in bed and was excited to soak in the tub, oil up my body and wear my sexy new bra with cut outs at the nipples and my open crouch panty combination. I had the water running in the tub while we ate so that I could jump right in when we were done.

I ended up not taking a solo dive in the tub as I planned, Tony decided to join me. He stepped into the bubble bath first and laid against the back of the tub, I stepped in after him sitting in between his legs. He took his hands and started rubbing my nipples from behind.

He whispered in my ear, "I love these big ass titties."

I closed my eyes indulging in his sweet touch. I felt his manhood growing on my back and he began kissing my neck and rubbing my breasts in a circular motion. I was hot and bothered and ready to get it on at this point. I knew that I wouldn't be wearing my new lingerie tonight, I was already naked, wet and horny. We stood to our feet and Tony took my sponge and filled it with liquid soap washing every inch of my body taking a little extra time with the sponge in between my legs slowly rubbing it up and down softly as my kitty tingled.

I grabbed the sponge from his hand and soaped up his muscular chocolate frame. Jail did my baby's body some good, he had hardly any body fat, his six pack, triceps and biceps were tight and solid as a rock. He wasn't overly muscular but he was just right. My petite frame and big titties were the perfect match for Tony, our body types complimented each other.

My hair had grown so much longer over the years and my long mane was always mistaken for a weave and my caramel complexion still held its youth as if I was still in my teens.

"You're so fuckin' dope," Tony said looking me up and down tucking in his bottom lip. He lifted me up to his waist and I wrapped my silky wet legs around his body and we commenced to kissing passionately and aggressively. He positioned my body to slide in his dick and I let out a deep moan as his dick penetrated my kitty.

Tony was thrusting my body back and forth on his dick as my legs gripped his waist and then he started bouncing our bodies up and down in a fast motion as we connected with each other enjoying each bounce.

"Fuck me!" I moaned as we continued to bounce.

A Hood Chick's Story Part II

Tony placed me down and he stepped out of the tub. He knocked everything off the hotel sink and all of the toiletries flew to the floor.

"Come sit that juicy ass over here," he demanded.

I went to sit on the edge of the sink with no hesitation. Tony spread my legs and rammed his dick inside of my already moist cat. As he was stroking he seductively looked in my eyes and asked, "So you want me to fuck you?"

"Yes!" I moaned.

"Tell me what you feel!" He demanded.

"I feel your big dick!"

"You feel what?" He rammed it in even harder.

"Uhhh!" I moaned louder trying to take it.

"I feel your chocolate dick."

Tony kept stroking and I kept moaning.

"Play with your titties," he said. I laid my back against the mirror and then I stuck my finger in his mouth and used his saliva to play with my nipple. I made him lick two fingers on the other hand and I played with my clit while he kept stroking. I knew how to please and keep Tony turned on. After all, he's the one that taught me everything I knew. I enjoyed being his freak just as much as he loved the freak in me.

After a little while, Tony quit stroking and opened the bathroom door to see if our daughter came outside of her bedroom. Once he saw that the coast was clear he waved his hand motioning for me to come on. I hopped off the sink and followed Tony to the bed. He laid down flat on his back, his manhood stood straight up. I wet my lips looking at how sexy he looked laying on the bed.

"Come ride Daddy's dick." I hopped right on with no hesitation and started winding my hips like a professional belly dancer.

"Hell yeah, keep fuckin' me," he said.

"Uhhh," I screamed out as I felt myself about to climax.

"Yeah Ashley, keep fuckin' me."

WAIT!! I KNOW I DIDN'T HEAR THIS NIGGA RIGHT! I jumped off his dick with the quickness interrupting his groove.

He looked up at me shocked, "Why you stop?" He hadn't realized what he had just said.

"You just called me Ashley, who the FUCK IS ASHLEY!"

"What! Girl your hearing shit, come sit back on my dick so I can bust this nut!" I sat on the edge of the bed and I faced Tony.

"You fuckin' someone named Ashley Tony?"

He became defensive. "You know what, fuck it! I'll go jack my shit off, you out here trippin' on some dumb shit!"

A Hood Chick's Story Part II

Suddenly he got up and stormed into the bathroom. I didn't know if I should be mad, start crying or what. Who the fuck was Ashley? I couldn't think of anyone by that name. I began thinking of all the times that Tony was out. When could he have had time to meet or fuck someone else, we were always together? He came home every night, we worked together, lived together, we were inseparable, the only time that we weren't together was when we spent time with our friends which was very seldom. I really hoped that I was hearing shit. I didn't want to break up our family for nothing. But I couldn't shake the fact that this nigga called me Ashley and at all times, it was when we were fuckin'!

I started getting myself worked up again hearing Tony's voice in my head call me Ashley and needless to say I was fired up. Tony and Shayonna was all that I had. I hadn't talked to my mom in years because she blamed me for the death of my little brother. My older brother was locked up doing ten to fifteen so I didn't have any place to turn if Tony was stepping out on me. I damn sure wasn't moving back into the projects with Renee. The intensity of it all caused me to get a migraine.

When I finally calmed down and collected my thoughts, Tony was finished handling his business in the bathroom. I was still sitting in the same spot at the edge of the bed with a puzzled look on my face. He sat next to me and put his arm across my back and grabbed me close trying to talk calm and sweet.

"T, I'm sorry, I don't know what the fuck I was thinking, what was that name that you said I called you?"

I turned to look at him like he was stupid because that's what he tried to play and I said, "You called me Ashley."

"Well, I don't know anyone named Ashley." He turned my head to face his. "Listen to me T." He gazed in my eyes with a serious look across his face. "You and my baby are my everything and I wouldn't jeopardize that. I don't know an Ashley and I'm not cheating on you a'ight?" He pulled my head to his face and kissed my lips. I was still upset and refused to kiss him back. I didn't know what to say to him, I was numb and remained silent.

He slipped on his boxers, got in bed and buried himself under the covers.

"Baby come lay down," he said.

I finally stood from the spot at the edge of the bed and slid under the covers to lay with unanswered questions. For the first time in our relationship, I didn't want Tony to touch me. Normally I couldn't sleep if I wasn't cuddled up under Tony but tonight was different. I didn't want his ass near me.

The next day the three of us got dressed and headed straight to Fifth Avenue. I wasn't my normal happy self and

A Hood Chick's Story Part II

it showed. I was usually excited to shop for Tony, the baby and myself. But I had other things flowing through my mind besides shopping.

"You okay?" Tony asked when he noticed me daydreaming while holding an article of clothing for Shayonna. I snapped out of my trance answering Tony with a lie. "Yeah I'm fine."

I picked up some True Religion jeans for Tony and found me some black Prada shoes and was ready to go. I wanted this New York trip to end so that we could get back to the Bean so that I could do my research to find out who Ms. Ashley was.

"Tony, we don't have to stay here another night, we can leave tonight so that we can be back in Boston by the morning."

"You sure baby?" he asked. "You don't want to do our normal routine, eat at Sylvia's again today and then dine at Justin's in the morning?"

"Not this time, I'm not feeling well, I rather us leave later tonight."

Tony knew that Justin's, P. Diddy's restaurant, was my favorite spot but I still had to shut him down. I wasn't up to staying and being around Tony any longer until I had answers. Countless thoughts were racing through my mind. Thoughts that only women who have been cheated on would think of doing. Things like going through his pockets or his cell phone. Now normally I was the chick who respected her man's privacy, but since he had now given me reason not to trust him, I was determined to secure his cell phone and look through it. I went from 100% trusting him to 100% not.

After shopping, we headed back to the hotel to get our things together to leave. Tony took down most of our luggage to the car while the baby and I were in the hotel room gathering up everything else.

Fortunately for me, Tony had left his cell phone charging on the nightstand. I picked it up and quickly went through it before Tony made his way back upstairs. I surfed through his call log to check his received and outgoing calls and sure enough right before my eyes were consecutive dates and times next to the name ASHLEY.

My heart dropped and my entire mind state was numb.

A Hood Chick's Story Part II

Chapter Two – My New Life With Tony

We had a quiet ride back to Boston. The only time that I spoke was when my daughter asked me a question. Tony tried his best to make small talk with me but I kept shit short and sweet. "Baby, what's wrong with you, you still don't feel good?"

I glared over at his pitiful ass from the passenger seat.

"No Tony, I don't, as a matter of fact I feel worse."

"Aw, alright sexy, when we get back to the Bean, I'll make you feel real good," he said sucking in both lips like LL Cool J but the sexy thug look wasn't working for him this time, I was disgusted with him because he was a fuckin' liar. I wanted to gag. He had the nerve to call me sexy and think that there was a chance of him fucking me when we got home; well he had another thing coming.

He claimed not to have known anyone named Ashley but he was talking on his phone with her just about every day. What the fuck could they have been talking about? I felt stupid and ashamed, I trusted this man and gave him my all, I felt betrayed but it wasn't unusual for some bullshit to occur in my life. I was like a poster girl for bad luck.

Luckily I memorized Ashley's number and I stored it in my phone. I planned to have a nice chat with her when we got back into town.

After the long dreadful ride back to Boston, we pulled up in the driveway of our home. Tony and Shayonna got out of the car and started unloading our bags out of the trunk. She loved helping her dad. I sat in the passenger seat anxious to call Ashley. I couldn't even wait till I got in the house. I wanted to speak to her ASAP. As soon as Tony and Shayonna let themselves in the house, I picked up my cell phone and called Ashley. I tapped my foot on the car floor as the phone rang hoping that she would hurry up and pick up before Tony came back outside.

"Hello?" The voice of a hoodrat who sounded as if she was twirling her weave braid with her finger and chewing on bubble gum pierced through the phone.

"Hello is this Ashley?" I asked.

"Yeah who dis?"

"Don't worry about all that. I found your number in my fiancé's phone and I was calling to see who the hell you were."

A Hood Chick's Story Part II

"Excuse me, your fiancé?"

"Yeah, my fiancé," I repeated. "My fiancé Tony."

Ashley chuckled. "Tony? Girl Tony and I have been fuckin' for like two years and he never mentioned having a fiancée. He mentioned having a baby mama that he wasn't with anymore."

My heart almost dropped out of my body and rolled out onto the car floor but I wouldn't let Ashley hear my weakness. "Is that right? So how is it that y'all been fucking for two years and you didn't know that he had a fiancée? He's home every night so you must have been settling for seeing him for twenty minutes a day. That's the type of chick you are?"

"Ha, Boo you got it twisted. Tony be picking me up from work sometimes, buying me shit and letting me whip his Beamer."

My mouth fell to the ground, especially as I took in her last words.

"Whoa! Whoa! Whoa! Slow the fuck down," I said. "He be doing what and letting you whip what? Yeah okay bitch, so if you be seeing him so often, where do y'all be fuckin?"

"Oh he comes over here the majority of the time or we'll go to a hotel but we never stay the night."

LaShonda DeVaughn

"So if you knew the nigga never stayed the night out with you, why the hell wouldn't you think that maybe he had a fucking family at home to get too."

She interrupted me. "Wait before you start wilding out and disrespecting me, you can't point the finger at me for breaking up a happy home, I didn't know shit about you. Me and him were supposed to be on some exclusive shit. He told me he lived with his boy Shawn. He got a room and clothes and shit there so I thought it was his crib too."

My mind took off like a bullet out of an automatic pistol; I couldn't believe this asshole was living a whole 'nother life with this hoodrat bitch. I mean, I'm from the hood but I got class, this bitch sounded like she was a straight gutter bird brain bitch. At that very moment, Tony came back out of the house to retrieve more bags from the trunk. He walked over to the passenger side and tapped on the window and spoke through the glass.

"Baby, why you still in the car?" I looked at him with a face full of evil, if I could've spit at him through the window, I swear I would have. Within that second I put on my game face and devised a plan. I smiled while opening the door and I handed him my cell phone and said, "Baby, it's for you."

He pointed to himself, "For me?"

"Yeah," I said pushing the phone in his direction.

He took the phone from me and said. "Hello?"

A Hood Chick's Story Part II

"OH so you have a fiancé huh?" I could hear Ashley's loud ghetto mouth through the phone. Tony looked dazed as if he had just seen a ghost and he froze looking like he was shitting in his pants.

"What's wrong baby?" I asked sarcastically. He quickly tried to hang up the phone and I stood up out of the car and smacked the fuck out of him. "I thought you didn't know anyone named Ashley you lying ass nigga!"

He held his cheek. "Tiara if you ever put your hands on me again, I'll knock you the fuck out."

"Tony, I wish you would hit me, save your threats for Ashley. Don't get mad cause you got caught."

"How did you get her number?"

"Don't worry about all that." I sassed.

He poked out his chest and brought out the cockiness in his tone.

"You know what? Shayonna told me that you was looking in my phone when y'all were in the hotel in New York." He tried to grow angry and switch the blame on me like a typical nigga.

"So you're looking through my phone now? What the fuck T, that shit is corny!"

"Don't try to switch it Tony, you told me that you didn't know anyone named Ashley but you've been talking to the bitch every day. You told that ho that you live with

31

LaShonda DeVaughn

Shawn and you let her drive the fuckin' car that's in my name? And you be taking this bitch to hotels?"

"She's lying T, you know she's lying because I come home to you every night," he said skipping over everything else that I asked.

"Nigga just because you come home every night doesn't mean you're not fuckin' the next bitch on your spare time.

Tony threw the bags on the ground and walked over to the driver's seat.

"Well fuck it then, you don't fuckin' believe me, I'm out, I don't have time for this shit."

I stormed behind him. "Tony how the fuck you gonna try to bounce and not answer why you lied about knowing her?" I screamed.

"So you fucked her Tony?" He didn't answer me. He opened up the driver's side door and sat in the car. I tried pulling on the door so that he couldn't close it."

"Answer me, you fucked her didn't you?"

The bass in his voice echoed loudly. "T, get the fuck off the door!"

"No! Answer me Tony!" I kept tugging on the door until he became irritated and he yelled even louder.

"Get the fuck off the door Tiara!"

I finally gave up only because I didn't want the neighbors to pry and I let him shut the door.

32

A Hood Chick's Story Part II

"Well fuck you then Tony, it's over!" I screamed as he peeled off.

Shayonna came running out the house.

"Mommy where is daddy going?"

I started crying hysterically and I grabbed Shayonna while he sped away.

"Come on baby, let's go in the house."

Shayonna's eyes were glued to my face. "Mommy, what's wrong?" The worry in her innocent face exceeded.

"Nothing baby, come on."

I led her in the house and I broke down immediately. I didn't have the strength to walk my daughter to her room. I broke down right in front of her. Everything from my past that I kept buried inside of me came pouring out.

"Mommy, what's wrong, why are you crying?"

I sat at the kitchen table and stretched out my arms and put my head down. "Baby just go to your room okay?"

I could hear her voice start to get squeaky, she didn't understand why I was crying and she hated to see that I was hurt. She gently rubbed my back with her young hands.

"Mommy did daddy do it?"

I raised my head and took her into my arms.

Shayonna thought the world of her father and I would never steal her joy.

"No baby, Mommy's just not feeling good."

LaShonda DeVaughn

While embracing my daughter, I felt her love, genuine, real, authentic love that no man in this world could offer. I had to put my emotions aside and had to be a mother first.

I wiped my tears, got myself together and I prepared her a meal. Later, we went upstairs and I readied her for bed. I ran her bath water and put her in the tub and then prepared her clothes for school in the morning. While she was playing in the tub, I went in my room and stared at myself in the mirror. I looked deep into my own eyes and wondered what the fuck I did wrong. I pleased Tony physically and mentally. I was a freak in the bedroom; I ran his business like I had been in the real estate game for years and we barely argued. I cooked and cleaned, what the fuck else could he have wanted that I couldn't offer? I been through too much in my life, I just knew that I left all drama in my past and that Tony was my savior from it all. This couldn't be happening to me. New bullshit was unwelcomed.

My thoughts were interrupted by my daughter yelling from the bathroom.

"Mommy, I'm done."

"I'm coming baby."

I dried her off, applied her lotion, threw on her PJ's and she tucked herself in bed.

"Good night baby." I planted a kiss on her plump cheek and I went to turn the light out.

A Hood Chick's Story Part II

She stopped me before I left out of her room. "Mommy?"

I turned, "Yes Baby."

"Is Daddy going to kiss me goodnight too?"

Her voice melted my heart and I swallowed a gulp of my pride trying to fight tears.

"Yes baby, he will kiss you goodnight too."

I left my baby's room hoping that I didn't just lie to her. I didn't want to see Tony's face but I wanted him to come home for Shayonna's sake.

I cleaned out the tub and ran my own bathwater. I wanted to soak and think. I turned on my old Beyoncé CD and pressed repeat on number six, Me, Myself and I and I started applying the lyrics to my own life situation. Me, Myself and I was truly all that I had to depend on because everyone that I loved in some form had let me down.

I sat in the tub drinking from the bottle of Chardonnay soaking myself in more tears than bath water. I turned on the bubbles to the let the Jacuzzi tub massage my body and relax me.

I cried so hard, you would have thought someone was killing me. I knew that I was stuck, everything we built together was for us. I never came into this thinking that I should have had a plan B.

I dried myself off, saturated my body in baby oil and laid on the silk sheets in our empty bed. For some reason that

35

night more than any other, the bed smelled more like Tony's Curve cologne making me sick to my stomach wondering if he was in Ashley's bed with her at that very moment.

I ended up crying myself to sleep and the next morning I woke up to the same empty bed, without Tony. I woke up my daughter and readied us both for school and work. As we were walking down the stairs Shayonna happily blurted, "I was so happy when daddy kissed me last night." I thought that she had to be dreaming until we got to the bottom of the stairs and walked past the living room.

He was passed out on the couch. I didn't even try to wake him up. I smelled the liquor on him all the way in the kitchen. I damn sure wasn't making him any breakfast. I made my daughter a bowl of cereal and I ate a nice bowl of stress thanks to him. I hadn't had an appetite ever since I had talked to Ashley.

I tried to sneak out of the house without saying a word to him but my baby ran up to the couch.

"Bye Daddy, I'm going to school." She placed a kiss on his cheek. He woke up, his eyes were barely open and he looked up at me.

"Why didn't you wake me up, what time is it?"

"It's eight o'clock," I said.

I didn't utter another single word, I grabbed Shayonna's hand and I walked out.

A Hood Chick's Story Part II

I dropped her off at school which her dad and I usually did together in the morning before heading to the office. But I didn't want him near me nor did I care if he was on time for work or not. I was the one that opened the office and prepped the staff in the morning anyway.

When I arrived at the office, I sat at my desk and stared at my blank computer screen. I didn't have the energy to do anything; I had too much on my mind. What was bothering me the most was the fact that Ashley said that they had been fucking for two years. Tony had only been out of jail for two years so I had to do a little bit more research on this bitch.

I called Renee, I didn't want to tell her what was going on so I had to think of a lie.

I just couldn't tell her about Ashley and Tony because she thought I was the luckiest chick in the world for having Tony but I wanted her to do some hood research for me and find out everything there was to know about Ashley. Boston was big, but people ran in tight circles. I knew that she was bound to know someone who knew her.

"Renee?"

"What up T? Why you calling so early?"

Renee's lazy ass didn't have a job. For as long as I'd known her she never had any work ethic. She wanted a man to take care of her and didn't mind staying with her mom until she found him. Most of her siblings moved with their fathers so she was the only old one in the house mooching off her mom.

"My fault, I didn't mean to wake you up, but I need a favor."

"What's up?"

"I need you to find out about a girl named Ashley. Find out where she stays, where she be at and all that."

"Who is she T? Do we have to beat her ass?"

I had to think of a lie quick! It was just too embarrassing to let my girl know that my man was fuckin' the shit out of another bitch.

"Um, nah nothing like that. One of the girls that work here at the office found out that she was fuckin' with her man so she asked me to find out about her."

"So you don't know how she look or nothing?" Renee asked.

"Nah, I just know she's mad ghetto. Oh and I heard that Tony's friend Shawn knows her, maybe you can try to get some info out of him. But make sure he don't tell Tony that you're asking. You know Tony will just tell me to mind my business and to let this chick do her own research, you know how he is."

"Yeah I know. A'ight, well I'll ask Shawn's cousin Tyrone, he's one of them gossiping ass niggas so he probably knows something and then I'll holla back at you later okay?"

A Hood Chick's Story Part II

"A'ight cool, thanks."

"No problem T, but I'll call you later, a bitch is tired, I'm going back to sleep."

"A'ight girl, talk to you later."

Renee was a good manipulator, she could smuggle some info out of Shawn or his cousin easily, she had the gift of gab. So I hung up with her and waited.

An hour later, Tony came in to work. He headed straight for his office. His clothes were wrinkled because I hadn't ironed them for him and he looked tired and annoyed and it was hilarious to me. I even snorted a giggle as he walked by because he looked totally dismantled. I shuffled through my paperwork pretending not to see him. The other workers greeted him and he ignored them all and slammed his office door behind him. He put down his briefcase and then opened the door calling out for me.

"Tiara can you come here for a second please?"

I walked in his office. "Yes Tony?"

"Baby, I couldn't find my tie that goes with this suit or my Armani belt. Do you think you can go home and get them for me? I have a client to meet today." His face read desperation and I just looked at him pitifully and realized that this man was nothing without me. And he must have lost his mind to think that I was going to be helping his ass out today.

LaShonda DeVaughn

I kindly looked at him and said, "Maybe Ashley can find them for you." I turned around and walked back out of his office. Tony walked up behind me and before I could sit down, he snatched my arm and yanked me out the office. Everyone looked up at us but I tried to crack a smile pretending like everything was okay.

When we got outside, Tony was furious and he squeezed tightly on my arm. "Tiara, I told you that bitch was lying to you. Yeah I admit, I may have lied about knowing someone named Ashley but that was because she is no one to me!"

I snatched my arm from him.

"Bullshit! How could she be no one if you're talking to her every fuckin' day?"

"I don't talk to that bitch everyday!" He griped confidently.

"Nigga, I looked in your call log, you talk to her enough. Why are you in my face still lying? Where did you meet her at to Tony? She said y'all was fuckin' around for two years, two fuckin' years yo!" I pushed him away from me and folded my arms.

Tony took a deep breath and was fuming with anger because he was being forced to confess.

"Okay T, here's the truth. When I got out, I hooked up with her on some business shit. She sells weight and I was using her connects."

A Hood Chick's Story Part II

"Business my ass Tony, so when did it turn into pleasure?"

"I only hit it one time I swear. One day me and you had an argument and I was vulnerable, she was always ready to throw the pussy at me so that one time I took it."

"So every time a nigga get caught up they claim to only hit it once? Tony that's straight up bullshit, do I look stupid? Do I look like one of these dumb ass bitches out here? And what is this shit about you telling her that you live with Shawn?" I was letting it all out on Tony with no chaser.

"Yeah I did tell her that," he admitted. "I don't trust that bitch, I wasn't telling her where we lived."

"*And* you be spending money on her bringing her to telly's and letting her whip your car? You making me look like a damn fool Tony!"

Tony looked at me shaking his head. "Damn that bitch was on the phone running her fuckin' mouth like it was really that serious."

"Well it must have been that serious if it's been going on for two years." I cut my eyes at him, I was disgusted.

"A'ight T, she did drive my car once, it was when I was still hustling. She picked up some weight for me. I didn't want to drive with that shit in the car so I had her do it for me. You know I don't like to be too hot, and I had copped mad shit that day. She's stupid T, one of them chicks

41

LaShonda DeVaughn

that would do anything for a nigga. And we only went to the hotel that one time when I hit it."

He sounded convincing but I wasn't your ordinary naïve broad and I knew that a nigga would say anything to keep his family. They would lie until they were blue in the face and swear on everything they loved and some more shit just to make you believe them. But I also knew that bitches lie too. Especially when they know that they are just sideline smut ass bitches who would never be the nigga's number one.

Even though Tony was supposedly explaining his whole other life that was new to me up until forty-eight hours ago, coming clean wasn't good enough. I needed some time to think about if I wanted to forgive him or let him go. I mean, besides Derek, my first love who was taken away from me by murder at such a young age, Tony was the only other man that I had ever opened my heart to. Yeah I know it sounds stupid but I loved him and hoped that this shit wasn't that deep. I knew no other chick could replace me in Tony's life but just knowing that he was sneaking around on me made me feel so stupid.

Derek had slept with my best friend and I ended our relationship immediately but it felt different with Tony. I had a child with him and after losing close bonds with so many people in my life, I felt like he was all that I had besides myself. I was never one to let weakness get to me, but I had

42

A Hood Chick's Story Part II

a soft spot for Tony and this feeling wasn't me though, this feeling wasn't T, I was tough as bricks and now I felt weak. I knew that I needed time to get my head together because I'd put in too much work to let this man get over on me. I needed some space to think.

Tony looked at me, my arms were still folded and I was looking at the ground. He walked toward me. I had always known him to be cocky and overbearing but now his ass looked pitiful and sympathetic. He knew he fucked up, he fucked up bad. He tried to show in his face that he was sincere. He grabbed both of my arms and tried to look in my eyes. I lifted my head from the ground to look at him.

"T, I'm sorry, it will never happen again. You know how much you mean to me, don't let this hoodrat bitch break up what we have."

"Tony, if this is the end for us, always remember that it was YOU that let this hoodrat bitch break up what we had. I didn't stick your dick in her, you did."

He looked at me all stupid and pitiful like I was supposed to embrace him and tell him not to let it happen again. He had the wrong chick.

Suddenly an old Acura Integra sped up in front of us and this ghetto bitch jumped out of the car.

"Tony!" She squealed walking in our direction..

I began walking toward her and the old Tiara surfaced early!

LaShonda DeVaughn

"Who the fuck are you?" I asked

She stopped walking and answered me. She was moving her head like it was gonna fall off her neck.

"I'm Ashley."

A Hood Chick's Story Part II

Chapter Three – Plan B

When Ashley stated who she was, I looked back at Tony and then turned back in Ashley's direction and continued walking toward her. I was going to beat the shit out of her. She actually had the nerve to show up at me and my man's place of business. This bitch had the game wrong. When Tony snapped out of his state of shock, he ran in front of me realizing what was about to go down.

He snatched me up. "Come here T!"

He managed to push me behind his back but I was fighting to confront Ashley. He had a firm grip on my hands like he was a police officer about to put me in cuffs. Ashley was standing with her hands on her hips hollering. "Let her go, she wanna fight me because her man comes to me, then let her dumb ass go."

At that point I tried to smuggle my way in front of Tony with all my might but he knew that if he let me go, then it would have been a wrap for Ashley. She came out her mouth a little bit too much to the wrong chick. I screamed from behind Tony's back as I was tussling to break away from his grip.

"Bitch, trust me, you don't want him to let me go. You came to my place of business looking like you made that whack ass dress out of a pair of curtains and you don't think you're gonna get your ass whipped? You got me fucked up. Stay in a sluts place bitch, whatever you did with my man was done because you were convenient, go fuck with the next chick's man because you'll always be someone's number two."

Ashley was countering a whole lot of bullshit back at me and continued to play tough because she knew that Tony wouldn't let me go so the bitch kept popping off at the mouth.

"Please believe, Tony wasn't complaining when I was meeting him up here before, or maybe those were the days when you weren't working," she said sarcastically.

In my mind I was thinking, no this muthafucka didn't have this bitch coming up here for lunch but I wouldn't let her know that the shit she was saying was getting to me so I cut her short.

"Bitch, fuck all that! What the fuck are you coming up here for today?"

Tony asked her the same question, "Yeah, why the hell are you up here?"

"Don't play dumb Tony, you know why I'm up here. She peeked at me.

A Hood Chick's Story Part II

"So you must be Tiara, are you wifey Boo?" she asked trying to be funny,

I tried to compose myself and asked Tony calmly. "Baby, can you please let me go? I just want to talk to Ashley for a second."

That shit didn't work, Tony wasn't letting my ass go for shit. He knew that I was boiling at that point and if he would have let me go, I would have dug all in Ashley's ass.

"Tony, let this bitch know something for real," I demanded.

Tony was pissed.

"Ashley, you know this is my fiancé, I don't know why the fuck you was telling her all types of lies and shit. You need to be the fuck out, don't come back up here!"

Ashley chuckled and began walking back to her car talking shit. "Tiara you can believe him if you want to, he'll keep coming back, trust me. He must not love you and his little family too much as much time as we spend together."

She sat in her car and rolled down the window and put on her fake Chanel glasses, "I'll holla." She sped off and Tony finally let me go.

I started pounding on his chest with my fists as hard as I could as if he was Ashley.

"So that's the bitch that you only fucked one time? I can't believe this bitch came up here telling me that she be spending mad time with *my* man! Do you know how that feels to a woman? You let another bitch have what's mine you fuckin' asshole? Get away from me right now Tony I hate you!"

I took a deep breath, my heart was thumping and I was so hurt but I somehow calmed down a bit.

"You know what, it's over, this isn't a light wound here Tony, this cut is deep. You got yourself deep in a situation and got a bitch head over heels for you *and* she knows where you work. There is more to this and I'm not sticking around to find out. I'm taking the baby and I'm moving out."

Tony looked dumfounded but he let me talk the whole time without interrupting me. He sat there like a typical nigga who got caught up and didn't know what the fuck to say. As soon as he heard me say I was taking the baby and leaving it got his cheating ass attention quick.

"You ain't taking my daughter nowhere."

"Watch me," I said.

I went back into the office, snatched my purse off my desk and told them I was going to be gone for the remainder of the day. I assigned my assistant Susan in charge of all duties that I was supposed to take care of for the day and I left. Tony watched me from his office as I walked out. He stared at me with his face twisted up like he wanted to fly my head off and I sashayed out of the door.

A Hood Chick's Story Part II

I got into my car without a single destination in mind. Who the hell was I fooling, I didn't have anywhere for me and my daughter to go if I were to really leave Tony. I drove around thinking and sobbing. My ass knew there was more to Tony's relationship with Ashley. I knew that he would never leave me for her but just the thought of him fooling around with someone, spending time with another chick and making her think that she was something special to him was enough to hurt me, enough to hurt any woman. I questioned the depth of their relationship. How did she know where he worked? Tony was so secretive and private when it came to outsiders, why after all these years was he getting sloppy? I thought back on the times when I used to wonder where Tony was when he took long lunch breaks or had so-called lunch meetings that lasted until the end of the day that I didn't remember scheduling. He must have been with Ashley all those times. I felt like shit and I was a straight mess at that point.

I was Tony's Queen, how the fuck could he do this to me? Ashley was ghetto as hell but she wasn't that bad looking. She wasn't a dime or anything but she was decent. He told me that she didn't have a job because she got fired so she hustled which meant that she was convenient to have access to at all times of the day. While I bust my ass at the office, this jobless bitch was convenient enough to be around to let Tony have his way with her while my faithful dumb

49

ass was grinding for our family putting in the work for *his* business. I cried while banging on the starring wheel, how the fuck could he give my love away to some hoodrat bitch who wasn't worth standing in the presence of what's mine. This shit really hurt me, he betrayed me in the worst way and I didn't deserve this.

My cell phone startled me. I picked it up and it was Renee calling me back. I wiped my tears and tried to sound like everything was cool.

"Hello?"

"What up T?"

"What's up Renee, did you find out anything on that chick Ashley?"

"Yeah girl umm." She paused.

"I hate to say this T but I found out that that bitch is fuckin' with Tony hard. I heard that when he got out, he linked up with her and they have been messing around ever since. You sure she was fuckin' someone's man from your office or was it your man she was fucking?"

I couldn't lie anymore, I was caught. I should've known Renee would find out more than I asked.

"Yeah Renee," I admitted. "I found out that she was fuckin' with Tony. She even told me herself. I didn't want to tell you because the shit is embarrassing ya know?"

"I feel you girl but you don't have to hold anything from me, especially some shit like this, this is the perfect time where your friends come in at. But honestly, I'm not surprised at all. A nigga is gonna be a nigga. But you wifey so don't even worry about that smut, he don't want her."

"It ain't the fact of him wanting her or not, he wasn't supposed to be stepping out on me ya feel me? Matter fact, she just came by the office on some disrespectful shit, she straight crossed the line with me."

"What!" Renee shouted. "T, I found out where she lives so you just give me the word and we'll be over there ASAP. I hope you beat her ass?"

"Nah, Tony was holding me back. She was poppin off at the mouth and I wanted to tear her ass up. She was talking good shit too, then after a while she got in her car and left. I told Tony that I was good with him and I bounced out of the office. But girl, I was talking out my ass, I don't have nowhere to go."

"Well you know you always have me." She offered.

"I know you got my back but I can't move my daughter back in the projects. Shit is starting to get hot around there again and she don't need to be around all that."

"So what are you gonna do?"

"Good question. I was thinking of just going to the crib, packing up some shit for me and the baby and check in at a hotel and for a few days."

"You know that nigga's gonna go wild, with wifey gone *and* his daughter? Man listen!"

"Fuck him, let his ass go crazy, I don't want to see him right now."

"I feel you T, well just call me if you need me for anything, you know I got you."

"No doubt, thanks girl, I'll call you later."

I pulled into the driveway of my house and headed straight upstairs to pack up some clothes for me and Shayonna. I called the Holiday Inn and made reservations for three nights. I grabbed my Louis Vuitton duffle bag and stuffed our clothes inside. I left the house just in time to pick up Shayonna from school.

"Hi Mommy!" She said cheerfully getting into the car.

"Hey Baby, how was your day?"

"It was good, I had fun at recess."

"That's good baby, you got any homework?" I asked.

"Nope, I did it before we left, it was easy, it was my favorite subject, math. One plus one is two, two plus two is four…"

I felt so bad as my mind drifted away from my conversation with my daughter. I was wondering if Tony called Ashley. If they still had something going on and if he was going to use my time away to be with her. This shit was stressing me something bad.

A Hood Chick's Story Part II

"Why are we at a hotel Mommy?" Shayonna asked as I was checking us in.

I knelt down to my daughters level, "We are going to stay here for a few days 'kay'?"

"Is daddy coming?"

I stood back up to my feet. Her daddy questions were starting to become more and more painful. As I looked at her I wondered how he could risk losing our family and risk not living at home watching his daughter grow. I felt like he was selfish and plain dumb and I was starting to dislike him even more.

The hotel clerk handed me our room key and we walked toward the elevators.

"No baby, Daddy isn't coming." I finally replied.

She grinned poking out her bottom lip and I knew just the thing to cheer her up.

"They got a swimming pool here, me and you can go swimming."

Her face lit up and she smiled. "Yaay, did you bring my swimming suit?"

I smiled, "I sure did baby."

We went into our suite, got settled in and changed into our swimwear. I spent the entire night with my daughter worry free.

After swimming, she occupied my time by telling me about her friends at school, she showed me some of the steps she learned from dancing school and continued to be the sweetheart that she was. It was amazing at how smart she was. She was blossoming and getting older and it showed in her conversation. She was already a very intelligent student and took school very seriously. I wondered if she knew how much she meant to me.

I lost everything five years ago and God blessed me with her and I felt like she filled the void that was left when I lost my family. So many people had let me down throughout my life and this was the one person who was purely innocent and loved me unconditionally. I made a vow to myself that no one else mattered and it was all about my daughter and me.

I turned off my cell phone and when I turned it back on in the morning, I had about fifteen messages from Tony.

"Baby, where you at call me? Stop playing T call me! Okay T, I'm getting mad as shit now."

I deleted all of his messages and went on about my day. I dropped Shayonna off at school and I called Susan at the office and told her that she was in charge again and that I'd also be taking off two more days. She agreed to take care of everything but she told me she needed my help with some bills so I told her that I'd handle everything when I saw her and I headed back to the hotel.

Susan was cool as shit. She was a very bright and articulate young white girl from South Boston. I hired her

A Hood Chick's Story Part II

because she had years of experience working with various mortgage lenders as a loan originator. Her father worked for the Boston Police Department and I knew that she would be a valuable asset to our company because she possessed a lot of skills that we needed to keep our small business afloat. Her and I were like each other's mentor and we learned a lot from each other.

When I got back to the Holiday Inn, I laid on the cold hotel bed pondering my future; I needed a plan. I needed something stable for Shayonna and me, something fool proof and permanent so that I wasn't depending on Tony. I beat myself up for putting my all into a man and depending on him like shit would last forever. I thought I was living the hood fairytale, my drug dealer boyfriend turned legit. We were engaged and he once treated me like a Queen. Who would have ever thought that I would get shitted on.

I realize now that he was like every other selfish, cheating ass nigga and this was one lesson I'll pass on to my daughter, never put all your eggs in one basket. And more importantly NEVER depend on a man. But I guess I had blindfolded myself thinking that what we had was deeper than what it really was. He knew what all I had been through, I thought that he would always have me up on a pedestal and let no one come between us and no more heart break float my way. I was dead wrong, but lesson well learned.

One thing came to mind that I knew would certainly set myself and my daughter's future straight and that was property. I knew how to get the lowest interest rates and after being in the business for a few years, we even had connections with foreclosures. All the money that I had saved since Tony paid all the bills was going to help me finally gain some stability. It wasn't much, it was a good fifteen grand but I was going to use a FHA loan program so that I would only have to put three to five percent as a down payment. There was no better time to start than now.

I called in the office to talk directly to Susan and she told me that Tony was a wreck and had been asking about me all morning. She reminded me again about the pending bills that she needed help with but I disregarded the bills and told her not to let Tony know that I was on the phone. I made her take out the foreclosure list to find me something in Quincy that looked luxurious but was reasonably priced. She found a three family home for two hundred thousand dollars and from the details didn't need much work. *Jackpot!* She gave me the address and I left to go and view it.

It took me no time to locate the house and when I did, the real estate agent for the property allowed me inside to examine it closely. The house had minor cosmetic work that needed to be done. The porch needed to be painted, some of the floors needed to be shellacked and some of the moldings needed replacing but other than that, tenants would be able to move in right away.

They were all three bedroom apartments and the way the market was in Boston, I would be able to get two thousand dollars in rent off each floor. The mortgage payment on a two hundred thousand dollar loan would be somewhere like seventeen to eighteen hundred a month with taxes and insurance included if I got a good rate. Nothing was stopping me. I was buying this house and coming up. Houses like these were worth about four hundred grand so that was two hundred G's in equity already. It was a gold mine. I smiled at the thought of my daughter and I being well off without Tony. I spent that day signing and faxing my offer letter and contingencies and set everything up with Susan for a good program and hoped that if all went well, I could close on that house in thirty days.

Day three at the hotel and a few more hundred messages from Tony later and I actually wanted to go home. I was still angry at him but I missed him. I told myself that when I went home I would keep my guard up and only focus on what I had to do to move my daughter and me away from Tony. He wasn't going to be playing me and thinking he could get away with it. If it were that easy, he would do like any other nigga would, continue to fuck with both of us thinking that all he would have to do was say sorry and I would keep forgiving him once he got caught.

I packed up all of our clothes at the hotel and we headed home. Tony's car was in the driveway so I knew that I was about to be interrogated as soon as I got in the house. I opened the door and my daughter dashed past me and flew to her father's arms. He bent down to embrace her hugging her as if he hadn't seen her in years.

"How's my little Mama doing? Daddy missed you, where have you been?"

"We were at the--"

I immediately intervened.

"Shayonna, go upstairs to your room and let me talk to your daddy for a second."

Tony glanced at me curiously and my daughter looked at us both strangely and went upstairs, she was still unaware of what was going on between us.

"So where were you? I know you got my messages, how you gonna leave like that Tiara? That shit ain't cool." His words were as arrogant as usual.

"Why do you think I left Tony? Don't play dumb." I threw my keys on the counter and we both looked at each other in an awkward silence.

"Were you able to be with your little girlfriend during your free time away from me?" I asked.

A Hood Chick's Story Part II

He walked over to me, butterflies danced in my stomach because I thought that he was going to lash out on me and bring out the cockiness he used to set his business partners straight. Those situations were never pretty. Instead, he held my hand and got on one knee. He looked up at me and pointed to my ring.

"Do you know why I gave you this?" He said staring directly into my eyes.

"I gave you this ring because you are who I want to spend the rest of my life with." His eyes began to gloss and tears started falling from them.

I didn't know if it was an act to get me back or if it was sincere. Niggas went to drastic measures like crying crocodile tears to make their girls think that they were sincere so I kept my game face on for as long as I could.

"You and my daughter are my world. I may have fucked up but nobody's perfect. I'm manning up and letting you know that I made a mistake and I would never, ever, break your heart again. The three days that you were gone felt like eternity, it felt like someone was choking me and when y'all came walking through that door, I could breathe again. You're my Queen Tiara, my rock, my better half. I love you more than words can say."

My eyes watered and my tough act faded away. I missed him so much, he was my everything and it actually hurt to see him hurting. But I knew that he deserved every

LaShonda DeVaughn

fuckin' tear that he cried. He deserved to be hurt, punished and dismissed. But on the other hand, he was manning up, so maybe it was okay to give him a second chance. Seeing such a dominant man like Tony crying always seemed sincere.

And if it wasn't, I was surely about to find out.

A Hood Chick's Story Part II

Chapter Four – Too Many Lies

I found myself spending day and night thinking of ways to please Tony. I went to Copley and splurged at Victoria Secret buying every kind of lingerie they had. Tony loved me in thongs so I wore a different color and different style thong every night. I started role playing buying kitty cat and nursing outfits stripping down to nothing to keep it spicy in the bedroom.

He loved the nurse outfit the best because he would play my sick thug who was hurting in every place that he wanted me to put my mouth on. I mean, I gave this man all of me. I even bought a stripper pole and danced exotically for Tony to various R&B songs, I was going all out. One night him and I went to a strip club together in Providence and I recorded all of the stripper's dance moves in my mind so that I could put on even hotter shows at home for Tony. I sat confident with him in the strip club and was okay with them big booty bitches shaking their ass in front of him, it was cool because he was coming home with me.

LaShonda DeVaughn

We recorded ourselves making love in different positions. Sometimes we'd record ourselves having wild, crazy, porn star sex on every piece of furniture in our bedroom including the floor.

He purchased a Polaroid camera and took pictures of each and every one of my body parts and I posed for them all as if he were a professional photographer. I did everything to keep Tony anticipating making love to me. I tried to make sure to satisfy his every desire. I even went against the grain and gave him some dookey love. Yes, I let him stick it in my ass.

We connected sexually and mentally and it felt like we were closer than ever before. It's funny how cheating can make both parties realize their love for one another. Tony was mine and the fact that I forgave him made me even more territorial over him.

We signed my daughter up for a new advanced dance school and we attended all of her shows together. We were the perfect family again, everything seemed to go accordingly and Shayonna loved having us all together.

I sometimes questioned why I was going all out to please him since he was the one that fucked up, but I just figured that a woman was supposed to please her man in all forms anyway. I kept myself in check about checking Tony's phone. If I was going to start to trust him again I had to at least try to do it a hundred percent. That was until I noticed

A Hood Chick's Story Part II

that he started having late meetings again and too many club nights out with Shawn.

My phone rang around one in the morning on a Saturday. I was up folding clothes and Shayonna was already in bed sound asleep.

"Hello?" I answered.

"T, where is Tony?"

"Renee, I can't hear you with all that music in the background."

"Can you hear me now Tiara?"

"Yeah I can hear you."

"I was asking you where Tony was."

"Renee why are you asking me where my man is? He went to the club with Shawn, why?"

"That muthafucka went to the club alright. Girl I'm at the club right now and I just saw him and Shawn's black ass leaving out with Ashley and some other bitch."

I was hoping that Renee was mistaken and that maybe she had saw him leaving with a cousin of his or something, he just couldn't be doing this bullshit to me again. I threw the article of clothing that I was about to fold back into the basket and sat on my bed. It felt like my heart was beating through my shirt.

"Are you sure it was Ashley?"

"Oh trust me, it was Ashley, the DJ sent her a Happy Birthday shout out a little while ago and her funny looking

63

ass was letting it be known that it was her birthday too. She was all loud and sloppy and shit. That's how I spotted Tony and Shawn, they were with them in the VIP booth and after a while they got up and bounced.

"So where are they now?" I asked.

"Girl they drove off, I'm out here with my cousin Kathy, when I seen them leaving I tried to follow them outside but it was too late. You know I had no problems with snatching that bitch up if I would've caught up to them. And I would have checked Tony's ass for you too."

I didn't know what else to say to Renee because once again I was embarrassed. What I needed to do at that point was speak to Tony's bitch ass ASAP.

"A'ight Renee good looking out, I'll call you later, I'm about to call his ass right now.

"A'ight, one!"

I hung up with Renee fuming. Me putting in all that work for this nigga didn't mean shit! Overly pleasing him and giving him my all and here I was, shitted on once again. I felt like it was not even worth putting my pride aside to forgive him for cheating, forgiving him for embarrassing me and forgiving him for giving another ho my love. Renee was right, a nigga is gonna be a nigga and my thoughts right now were fuck niggas, all of them!

While Tony's phone continued to ring in my ear, I became infuriated with my own thoughts. He was really bold enough to leave the club with another bitch knowing there was bound to be people in the club that knew me and were probably happy that something shitty was happening to me. Tony was definitely gonna feel me.

Ring! Ring! Ring!

Several calls later and this nigga still didn't pick up the phone and I felt like I wanted to kill somebody. I flipped my phone closed and threw it across the room. I started pacing the room and ten thousand thoughts were rummaging through my mind. I went into our closet and started checking the pockets of all of his clothes. I was searching through some of his old jackets that he hadn't worn in a while; I just knew that I would find something.

To my surprise, I found two condoms, some naked photos of some bitch's body parts that weren't mine and I officially went coo-coo. My eyes enlarged in anger staring at photo after photo of some brown skin bitch's body and I fought hard to hold in my tears but it only turned into more anger and more rage. I looked at the condoms in my hand and gritted my teeth. Tony and I didn't wear condoms so who the fuck did he buy condoms for? I sat on my bed and let out a loud scream. I was more angry and disappointed at myself than I was with Tony. I should've let him go when I found out about Ashley. I gave him another chance trying to keep my family together and the shit backfired in my fuckin' face.

I wanted to wring his fuckin' neck. My cell phone finally rung a few minutes later; I ran over to answer it trying to fix the antenna that broke from me throwing it.

"Hello? Tony can you hear me?"

"Yeah I hear you baby, what you doing? Why you blowing up my phone?"

"Don't ask me what I'm doing, what the fuck are you doing and who the fuck are you with?"

"T, who the fuck you talking to? Calm that shit down, you know I'm out with my man Shizz. I'm gonna be out for a few more hours, then I'll be home."

"Oh really, well I'm on my way to Shawn's house to chill with y'all."

"Yo T, what the fuck is wrong with you man? You acting crazy, we just left the club a little while ago, we ain't even going to Shawn's crib. But I'ma holla back at you because I don't feel like arguing with you right now a'ight, One!"

Click!

Tony hung up the phone in my ear and I officially lost it. I called him back repeatedly and he didn't answer the phone. I wanted to pound in his fucking head. I contemplated whether to pack my shit or his and put him the fuck out. But then I thought about it. I couldn't do no Beyoncé 'To the left, To the left' shit because the house wasn't in my name. All I could do was start balling like a baby.

This was my life, my reality. I lost myself inside Tony. In the past I would never let someone get over on me so I started to feel a bit weak. I felt like I didn't have control over the situation and I had to do something quick. It hurt like death that someone who I loved so much was taking advantage of me. I didn't even know this man. This wasn't the Tony that I knew.

I checked on Shayonna to see if she was still asleep and she was still knocked out. I proceeded downstairs to wait for Tony to come home because I had some shit waiting for his ass.

Five o'clock a.m. rolled around and my ass was wide awake. I had pushed one of the kitchen chairs to the front door and sat anxiously waiting for Tony's arrival. I had the naked photo's scattered on the floor in front of me along with the two condoms. In my hand I held a large butcher's knife. He was gonna give me some answers tonight.

I heard his car pulling into the driveway and I took a sip of the wine that I had been drinking all night since I'd gotten the call from Renee and I placed it back on the floor beside me. Tony stumbled in the door and looked at me.

"T, what are you doing still up?" His words slurred.

He flicked on the lights and looked down at the pictures, at the condoms and then the knife in my hand. He peeped my face, saw my nostrils flaring and the anger that had tensed my body.

"Who did you leave the club with Tony? I heard you left with that little bitch Ashley."

Tony's cocky ass didn't even answer me, he pushed the chair to the side with me still seated in it and headed for the stairs.

"Man, I ain't answering to shit."

"Oh you ain't answering to shit! You think this is a fuckin game, getting all cocky and tough because you got caught up."

I headed toward Tony with the knife to my side. I wouldn't dare stab him but I wanted him to know that I was serious. He turned around and took the knife out of my hand and threw it across the floor behind me. He grabbed me by my neck and started choking me against the wall. I was in shock but tried to fight my way out at the same time.

"Tiara, I don't have time for this shit, I am the man in this house! I take care of you, you don't do shit but sit around and look pretty. I told you I ain't cheating on you, you're starting to get on my nerves with this questioning me shit." He let go of my neck and I began gasping for air.

"Fuck you Tony!" I said catching my breath.

"What do you mean I don't do shit but look pretty? I run your fucking business, and handle all of your bullshit! But since I just sit and look pretty, you can be in charge of

A Hood Chick's Story Part II

the bills and making sure the mortgage is paid on time because I ain't doing shit for you anymore. You're just trying to stray from the subject. You were seen leaving with that bitch point blank. There's nothing that you can tell me to make me believe you right now. *And* you put your hands on me? I fuckin' hate you!" I punched him in the face and he reacted at the same moment and shoved me against the wall. I was kind of scared because I didn't know what else he would do, but being from the streets, I could never let someone put their hands on me and get away with it so I charged at him as if I could beat him.

"I hate you!!" I screamed pounding on his back as he tried to go upstairs.

My punches didn't affect him, he kept walking and I stopped fighting him and went to swipe all of the pictures and condoms off the floor and I ran upstairs behind him. He had already reached our bedroom and was peeling off his clothes. He went in our bathroom and turned on the shower.

"Why are you taking a shower? You just went to the club and chilled with Shawn afterwards right? Uh huh, you fucking liar, you had your dick in some nasty bitch's pussy, but you forgot these." I threw both of the condoms at his face but he waved me off.

"Tiara go to bed, you're drunk."

69

"I ain't drunk; I'm just stupid, stupid for giving your ass another chance. Matter fact, come here, and let me smell your dick."

Tony became enraged at my accusations. "Listen bitch, I told you that I don't have time for this shit!"

I looked at Tony as if he were a stranger; it was one shock after another that night. He never called me a bitch before; he never disrespected me in all the years we were together. I was beginning to think that I never knew who the real Tony was. Or maybe he was just now showing me who he really was and hiding himself throughout the years because of my brother Trè. Now that Trè was locked up, maybe he thinks that he can start controlling me. It was either that or he was letting his money get to his head in the worst way.

"Bitch, Tony? I'll show you a bitch!"

I picked up his Timberland boots out of the closet and aimed them at his head one at a time. I was trying to knock his head off his fuckin' neck. He charged at me trying his best to dodge the boots that were flying toward him. He snatched me up and smacked the dog shit out of me. I held my cheek in shock.

"Yeah I knew that would shut your ass up." He grabbed my shoulders and started shaking me.

"Tiara, nobody is cheating on you! I'm getting tired of this shit, you know how many bitches out there wish they

A Hood Chick's Story Part II

had what you have, why don't you realize you're the only one that I want, these other bitches out here are nothing to me. This shit is driving me crazy, why the fuck are you so insecure, it's beginning to turn me off."

I yanked myself away from Tony and picked up the naked photos that I had dropped while picking up the boots to throw.

"Insecure Tony? It has nothing to do with being insecure, it's about what's real, and you keep getting caught. Look at these fuckin' pictures, your dumb ass is getting too sloppy with your shit, your game ain't tight. All these years I thought your ass was faithful but I was just dumb enough to trust you. Are these pictures of Ashley? Which one of your hoes pictures you had stashed away in the house? The same house that you share with your family muthafucka? What you want to jerk your dick off to these pictures?"

I smacked Tony and dared him to smack me back.

"Yeah," I said. "You thought I was just gonna let you get that hit to my face and I wasn't gonna do shit Tony?"

Tony laughed. "T, you can't bring that fighting hood shit into our relationship, you can't beat me. All that tough shit and smart mouth goes out the window as of now. You're my girl, I'm the king, you have to start listening to me, and all that independent shit disappears when you're in a relationship."

71

LaShonda DeVaughn

I let out a huff. "I will NEVER let you, nor any man nor woman hit me Tony, you done lost your fuckin mind. Now stick to what I asked you, what bitch's body parts did you have stashed?"

Tony took the pictures out of my hands.

"T, these are pictures of you. And I only put my hands on you because you came at me with a knife." He put the pictures in our small trash barrel.

"You sound stupid Tony; I know what my ass and titties look like. And you know I wasn't going to stab you with that knife." I paused and looked over at Tony as if he were a stranger in my bedroom. "What the fuck happened to you Tony? You've turned into a lying, cheating, woman beating bastard. Where did all this shit come from?"

"I don't got time for this Tiara." He went into the bathroom locked the door and proceeded to take his shower. Tony may not have known but he was just pushing me closer and closer to official independence. To actually leave the club with a chick, have pictures of a chick in his possession and then accuse me of not doing shit for him but looking pretty turned me totally against him. It all added up and I felt unappreciated. As of that moment, I was done with keeping up with our bills at home. He would now have to keep up with the mortgage and everything else that we had to pay. Eventually he'd see how much he needed me because I knew that he couldn't handle the responsibility. Especially when I got on my feet to leave for good.

I turned off all of the lights in our bedroom and laid in the bed with my heart weighing heavy in my body. What hurt the most was that Tony probably thought he could get away with lying to me. Maybe he was cocky because he thought that I needed him and that I was trapped. Little did he know, I was not that bitch.

After taking his shower he approached the bed and stretched out next to me.

"T, you still up?" he asked.

I rolled my eyes as I faced the opposite direction and I didn't answer him. He put his head under the covers and found his way to my kitty and started eating the shit out of me, literally because he ate my ass too. He head dived into my shit like he was eating a watermelon whole. It was his way of admitting that he was wrong, his way of saying sorry without saying it. As he was French kissing my insides, slurping and licking my clit, I couldn't get into it. I looked up at the ceiling wondering if he had just left from fucking Ashley and maybe even eating her pussy too.

I pulled the covers up to look at his head sucking, winding and humming on my clit and then I pictured him doing it to Ashley and I was disgusted. I pushed his head back and he looked up at me knowing that I hadn't came yet. I didn't want him to finish. It normally felt so good and I

LaShonda DeVaughn

would want him to keep eating all night. Tonight, I had enough of Tony, he was such a disappointment; I finally realized I never knew who he really was and it hurt.

A Hood Chick's Story Part II

Chapter Five – It's On

I stopped going all out for Tony. Hell I didn't even get wet to his touches anymore however I was still dumb enough to fuck him raw. He constantly avoided the subject when I asked about him leaving the club with Ashley and I eventually pushed it to the side. I didn't let it go though; there was no way that Tony was going to get the best of me. When I told him that it was my own homegirl Renee that seen him at the club, he quickly dismissed her claims saying that Renee was all about drama and that she's just jealous of our relationship; typical guilty nigga responses. He even started attacking her character saying that she was a chickenhead bitch that wanted me as miserable as she was and that she would fuck him if she had the chance because he believed she wasn't really my friend.

Funny how much he had to say about Renee but didn't have shit to say in his defense of her literally seeing him leaving with Ashley.

My loan application was completed and everything was looking good as far as closing on the three family house.

75

LaShonda DeVaughn

It wouldn't happen in thirty days as I had planned because it was a little more complicated with foreclosures comparable to a standard sale but it was still moving along smoothly. I was also surprised that I managed to keep it all away from Tony the entire time and I planned to keep it that way.

A few weeks had gone by and although I had plans to leave Tony, I had to know if he was still messing with Ashley.

Anytime he went to the store, to a meeting, to tie his fuckin' shoe without me there, I felt like Ashley was somewhere around about to jump out the bushes and start fucking him.

"Have you talked to your little mistress lately?" I asked while we drove to work together early on a Tuesday morning after dropping off Shayonna.

The previous night Tony had worked a so-called late night shift when I knew that I had tied up all loose ends at the office for the night. He came home after midnight, so I knew he was out doing something.

"Tiara, don't start with this shit, it's too early in the damn morning and I'm not in the mood."

He grinned and proceeded to drive us to work. Coincidentally his phone started ringing and I picked it up to see who was calling because it was plugged into the charger in the dash and the phone read "A." When I saw that I picked it up immediately.

A Hood Chick's Story Part II

Tony's dumb ass thought by not putting in her full name that I wouldn't know what the fuck the "A" stood for. Like I said before his game was no longer tight.

"Hello?"

"Who is this? Where is Tony?"

"Who the fuck is this? Is this Ashley, you're still on my man's dick huh?"

She chuckled. "This must be Tiara, guess you haven't got the memo, your man keeps coming back to me sweetie, deal with it."

Tony sped to the nearest curb and pulled the car over. He stormed out and rushed over to the passenger side. He opened my door and yanked me out by my hair causing his phone to fold closed and hit the sidewalk. He slammed me against the car screaming in my face.

"I told you it was too early for this shit Tiara! You like drama and I'm tired of this hoodrat bullshit! Who the fuck told you to pick up my fuckin' phone, what the fuck is wrong with you?"

"Tony get the fuck off me, I'm tired of your shit! You keep illing on me every time you get caught. Don't be mad because I caught your mistress calling your fucking phone early in the morning, you're the one that has to explain this shit, I'm the one that should be mad right now not you."

LaShonda DeVaughn

Tony started shaking me and my body was thrusting back and forth on the car.

"Stop Tony! Get off me, you're hurting me!" I tried to pry his hands off my arms but he held them tightly as anger flashed across his face.

"Tiara, I swear I feel like punching you in the fuckin' face right now, if you don't trust me then leave me, I am not cheating on your stupid ass."

"Get your damn hands off of me Tony." He let go of me and walked toward the driver's side. "If you're not cheating on me Tony then why the fuck is your mistress still calling you? And you keep putting your hands on me over this bitch? I'm tired of her and I'm tired of you, maybe I will leave your cheating ass."

Tony rushed back over toward me and pinned me up against the car.

"Tiara I told you to shut the fuck up, I'm tired of your smart ass mouth, shut the fuck up about this or I'm gonna bust your shit wide open!" He had his fist balled up in my face and that was the first time I was actually scared and believed that Tony would hurt me so I decided to shut my mouth.

Flashbacks of episodes of my father beating on my mom entered my mind. Anytime my mom said anything that my father considered as "back talk" he would fuck her up sometimes leaving her unconscious. I couldn't believe that I

A Hood Chick's Story Part II

was now dealing with someone who actually reminded me of my dad. I never wanted to be in a relationship like my mom and dad had and that's what Tony and me were becoming.

I wasn't as weak as my mom though. I couldn't sit and allow myself to stay with someone like him for years. I knew that I deserved better although I now know that my mom stayed for love. It took me to get this old to finally understand how the love of a man could make you stay with him even if you knew shit was wrong. But I was stronger than that and it was a wrap for his ass, my plans for leaving him just weren't executing quick enough. I had to play my position until I could get myself and my daughter away from this bitch made nigga.

When we got back into the car all I wanted to do was start kicking him with my stilettos in his sides while he drove but I didn't want to get into a car accident. Plus as I said, I was shook! Tony wore a look of vengeance and I wasn't fucking with that.

We rode in complete silence on our way to the office. The only sounds were of cars passing by and horns beeping due to the traffic as we got closer to the office. I placed my elbow on the door window and leaned my head against my hand and looked out into the street. A young boy who had to be around sixteen or seventeen was riding his bike close to the car and I almost burst into tears. He had long silky braids and buttery caramel skin with puppy dog eyes. He resembled my little brother to a tee. Part of me wanted to reach out and snatch him off his bike and hug him. He kept his eyes on the road occasionally looking over at me probably wondering why I was staring at him so hard. I eventually ended up turning my head with my eyes consumed with tears as we passed the boy by. The pain of losing my little brother was just as fresh as it was the day he departed. The anniversary of his death was approaching and I always became super emotional around that time. The situation with Tony only added fuel to an already burning fire and I was just an emotional wreck.

We pulled up to the office and Tony tried to squash the beef with more lies.

He parked into a tight parking spot and spoke without looking at me.

"T, I don't know what she called me for but I am not fuckin' that girl. I would not do that to you, she is history and for the last time, I am not cheating on you. I only got frustrated because you didn't respect my privacy. I don't answer your cell phone so you should respect mine."

On that note I got out of the car and went inside. Tony was so full of shit I could almost smell it. I couldn't sit there and listen to his lies anymore. I didn't even reply to him. I just sped into the office mumbling shit under my breath because I wanted to hit him so bad. He took a bit longer to come out of the car, he was probably in there smoking a blunt but when he came inside, I was already seated at my desk. I really didn't get much done that morning, I bullshitted up until noon because I was stressed and I couldn't focus for shit. When noon hit, I was out. I usually worked through my lunches but today was different.

Tony walked by my desk and put some paperwork on it and I didn't even acknowledge him. I took my cell phone out of my Louis Vuitton clutch bag and dashed out of the door to call Renee.

"Hey T, what's going on?"

"Nothing, same shit. Me and Tony was beefing this morning over that bitch Ashley again."

I heard the aggravation in Renee's tone. "I'm about tired of hearing about her T, if this was back in the day we would have been set it on her!"

"I know Renee and I don't know why the hell I was sitting here trying to handle this like a grown woman because she has just as much to do with this as Tony. At first I figured she didn't know about me because he lied to her telling her that we broke up and shit. But now she knows that we are engaged and have a family and the bitch is still around. So now I feel disrespected and it's on, it's as simple as that. I'm ready to get at her in the worst way Renee."

"Girl, I'm about to put on my scarf and meet you at your job."

"Nah Renee, wait till after work so that I can have my daughter settled in the house and get shit together first then I'll come get you. But trust me, we are most def doing this tonight."

"A'ight cool, I'ma check and see if I got her correct address and it's whatever with that slut ass bitch. I'm over here stressing anyway, I need to release my anger somehow."

"Girl *you're* stressing, my ass is over here about to explode. What's your crazy ass stressing about?"

"A bitch is broke that's what," Renee said.

I giggled and then heard Renee's doorbell ringing in the background and then she rushed me off the phone.

"A'ight T, holla at me when you get off work, my bell is ringing, it's this nigga Tank I'm tryna get some money out that nigga."

I rolled my eyes and shook my head. "A'ight Renee I'ma call your stank ass later."

I took out my set of keys to Tony's car, hopped in and drove up to one of the beauty supply stores in Mattapan. I was browsing up and down the aisles looking for jet black hair dye and some expensive weave. I wanted to switch up my look and make sure that I stayed on point everyday to keep Tony on his toes. He knew I didn't rock hair weave so he would notice the difference off top. I wanted to keep him guessing and have him thinking that I could be out here doing me and maybe his dumb ass would change before I had the chance to leave his ass.

I handed a hundred dollar bill to the cashier at the beauty supply store and she handed me back a five dollar bill. I thought to myself, damn, I didn't know weave was that fuckin' expensive. But it was some fly ass human hair, 18-inches long and that shit was gonna look hot on me. I drove to my hairdresser's salon which was only a little further up from the beauty supply store and handed her the bag. I told her that I wanted her to do some exotic shit to my hair.

She pulled the hair out of my black bag and looked at me surprised. "Whaaat! Tiara wants some weave?"

Everyone was so used to me getting wash and sets or fresh blow dry's so this was something different that everyone would notice.

"A'ight." My hairdresser said looking at me. "I know exactly what to do. Take my appointment book out of my booth and put your appointment in there," she said as she put my weave back into my bag and continued to set the chubby girl's hair that sat in her chair. I booked my appointment and dashed back to work.

As I approached my desk, I noticed a yellow post-it note that read *"When you get back from lunch, come into my office so I can eat that cat."*

LaShonda DeVaughn

I crumbled the note in my fist and threw it in my garbage pail. I was about tired of his verbal and sexual apologies. I was just about tired of Tony altogether.

It was back to work as usual, I made a few calls to some clients, took care of a few emails, printed out some applications and sent a bunch of paperwork to our underwriters for review. Susan and I were still struggling with some of the bills that weren't matching with the company account. As I sat at my desk completing a form, a silhouette darkened the paper, I put down my pen and looked up; it was Tony hovering over me.

"Did you get my note?" he asked.

"Yeah I got it," I said as nonchalant as possible. I picked up my pen and continued to fill out the form. Tony snatched the pen from my hand.

"So you ain't gonna let me taste that sweet shit?"

"Tony I'm busy." I pulled out another pen from my drawer and Tony frowned his face at my rejection and walked back into his office. Apparently he got his feelings hurt so he grabbed his car keys and walked his pitiful ass to the front door. Before leaving he yelled out, "Send my calls to my cell. I'll be back before the end of the day."

I watched as the door swung behind him and let out a huff. On a normal day, I would think that he was going to meet a client or running a legitimate errand but now I only believed that he was going to see Ashley.

A Hood Chick's Story Part II

"I hope it's worth it!" I said to myself as if I was speaking to Ashley because I was gonna beat her like she owed me money.

It was hard to focus but I managed to keep myself busy up until five o'clock which was the time Tony came back. He peeked his head in the door as I was shutting down the office and told me that he'll be waiting for me in the car. I shut off all of the lights and dreaded that I had to ride home with him.

I slumped down in the passenger seat with my arms folded looking straight ahead. Tony hadn't put the key in the ignition. He just sat in silence looking at me. It was a very uncomfortable silence until he tried to playfully poke one of my folded arms.

"So you still mad at me T?"

I ignored him and continued looking straight ahead.

"Man, I don't know what I gotta do to show you that I don't want no one but you."

He put the key into the ignition and drove off.

"I got a suggestion, you could keep your dick in your pants," I shot back.

"Ha, ha, ha! Wow T, you really don't know how much I love you. You really be buggin'. I am not fucking no one else."

He let out a cocky sigh and shook his head. "What a nigga gotta do, bring you to the alter to show you I'm serious?"

I cut my eyes at him. "Tony you ain't marrying nobody." I glanced down at my ring and started playing with it on my finger.

"Man you probably just gave me this to keep me content while you were out there doing you."

"Damn T, give a nigga some credit. I gave you that ring because I love you, you're already my wife we are already married if you ask me."

"Oh no Tony we are not married, I didn't walk down no aisle and if we were married then you did a good job at committing adultery."

"Man, stop all that stupid talk. I love you and my daughter so much; I ain't shit without y'all, that's real talk. My family is all I have. And trust me baby, I don't be meaning to put my hands on you. It just seems like you start blitzing about something at the wrong time. A nigga be stressing and you over here asking who I'm fucking. I don't wanna hear all that bullshit ass drama all the time. You need to know who you are to me."

"You want me to know who I am to you Tony? Let me tell you what that means to me. To me that means 'Tiara, you are the one that I want to be with but I'm fuckin' other people.' So don't give me that shit. And since when have you been stressing? We tell each other everything, now all of a sudden when your dirt surfaces your claiming that you're stressed out?"

I waved my hand before continuing. "I don't want to hear it! I play my position, I take care of our child, our household and I was managing our finances so I don't see nothing for you to be stressing about."

"See that's because you have had this fucked up attitude lately and I don't want to talk to you about anything."

I shifted in my seat so that my back was to my door so that I could look at him while he drove.

"Do I have a reason to have an attitude Tony? Let me fuckin' remind you." I started naming shit on each finger. "I find out about your little mistress, you lie to me about knowing her. My girl peeps you leaving the club with her. I find naked photos and condoms and now the bitch is still calling your damn phone. How am I supposed to feel?"

He lit his blunt and took a puff.

"I hear you talking T but most of the shit you said are lies and a bunch of bullshit. She wasn't my mistress. I told you that shit was all about business and it's done. Those condoms and pictures weren't mine, they were Shawn's."

I shifted to sit in my original position because I couldn't look at this compulsive liar any longer. All of a sudden the condoms and pictures were Shawn's? Come on now. I wanted to rip his tongue out and throw it onto the street.

I couldn't hold back any longer so I brought his bullshit to the surface. "So the pictures and condoms are Shawn's now?" I shook my head. "Tony you never cease to fuckin' amaze me man, I can't take this shit straight up. It's like I was straight wasting my breath talking to you just now."

He reached over and put his hand on my thigh and rubbed it. "I love you baby, I'm sorry if I hurt you in any way. But you're making it bigger than what it is. I don't want that girl. If I wanted her then I would be with her. Nothing or no one would make me leave my family, remember that. I know what I have and I'll never let it go."

I sat amazed at Tony's compulsive lying. I was so pissed off and couldn't believe that I was going through some shit like this. He didn't own up to any fuckin' thing.

At this point in my life, I was supposed to be happy. I should be indulging in the new rejuvenated Tiara, not stressing. And from Tony's dumb replies, I could tell shit wasn't going to get any better.

We pulled up to our house the same time as Tony's aunt. She had picked up the baby for us since she got out of work early every other day.

I gave his aunt a hug and thanked her before she left and we all settled inside of our once cozy home. It was now

A Hood Chick's Story Part II

smothered with tension and animosity. I headed straight upstairs and Tony followed behind me rubbing my ass as if he wanted everything to go back to normal just like that.

"You cooking baby?"

I reached my hand to take his hand off my ass and said, "No!" And I rolled my eyes at him.

"T, you're still on that shit? How long are you gonna keep acting like this? It's getting old."

"Fuck you Tony," I said as I headed inside of our bedroom.

Shit was not going to go back to being lovey-dovey just like that. Not only was he still lying but who knows where the fuck he really went when he took that extended lunch break today. Everything that he did irked me.

He took off his suit and shoes and headed downstairs to do the usual. Either watch ESPN or play that damn video game. He was still too comfortable thinking that he had it made with just throwing lies at me and me not leaving him but it only revved up my adrenaline to fuck Ashley up more and to eventually leave his whack ass.

I changed my clothes and threw on my BCBG Velour sweat suit, my Diesel sneakers and then prepared my daughter a kid cuisine meal. I had to fix her something quick so that I could hurry up and meet Renee.

"I'm finished mommy."

LaShonda DeVaughn

I examined her plate; she had eaten all of her nuggets, her macaroni and cheese but picked over her vegetables.

"Eat some more of your peas baby."

"I don't like them mommy, I don't want no more."

"Just eat a little more for mommy baby."

"Aww man." She pouted.

Tony listened from the couch in the living room and decided to add in his two cents.

"She don't have to eat them nasty ass, fake ass peas, you shoulda cooked us a real meal."

I smirked at Tony but instead of getting mad I kindly suggested that he made sure that Shayonna was bathed and ready for bed before nine o'clock and he agreed. So I picked up my purse and headed for the door.

"Where are you going?" Tony asked.

"Nowhere," I said shutting the door behind me.

I hopped in my car, called Renee to tell her that I was on my way.

I was focused.

Ashley was finally about to feel me.

A Hood Chick's Story Part II

Chapter Six – Still Hood

When I arrived at Renee's house, she was already outside waiting but she looked a bit strange. She had on a baseball cap, a dark pair of glasses and she didn't pick her face up from looking down. I followed her with my eyes all the way up until she got into the car.

"Girl we are going to whoop someone's ass not a jewelry store heist. What up with the black hat and glasses?" I joked.

Renee got in the car, shut the door behind her and finally looked at me. She tilted her glasses toward her nose. Her right eye was swollen like someone had stuffed cotton balls inside and it was almost sealed shut.

"Oh hell no! Who the fuck did this to you?" I griped.

"Chill T, calm down." She put her glasses back on.

"It was that nigga Tank. I been fuckin' him for a month now and the nigga was acting cheap with his gwap. Not only that, but he was mad disrespectful with it talking about he ain't giving me shit. So I told him not to bring his raggedy ass to my crib anymore. I wasn't fuckin' his little dick ass for free. Plus I know his girl, me and her are cool."

I had to interrupt her. "Wait Renee you know his girlfriend and you're cool with her? Why are you fucking one of your people's man?"

"You know her too T, remember Bianca that used to babysit for you?"

"The little good girl?" I asked surprised.

"Yeah that's his so-called girlfriend. He got him a good girl but he be fuckin' around on her so after he kept poppin' off at the mouth I told him that I would tell his girl about us and that's when the nigga started tripping."

"I can't believe he put his hands on you, he forced it." I searched her entire face with my eyes when she took her glasses completely off. "Renee look at your lip, one side is swollen!"

"I know T, I ain't trippin'. I'ma have some nigga's see him."

"You damn right! I ain't got no sympathy for a cheater let alone a nigga that hits a chick. But you have to stop fuckin' with people's men, you're too old for that shit, you need to find you a good dude and settle down. You should be someone's wife not someone's ho."

"T, please don't start with that preaching shit."

"There is a difference between preaching and keeping it real, you're my friend, I wouldn't be real if I didn't tell you how I felt. I just want you happy, it's about that time don't you think?"

A Hood Chick's Story Part II

"Yeah, yeah I know," Renee said disregarding me.

I took the key out of the ignition and Renee quickly sat all the way up in her seat.

"Why you stop the car?" she snapped.

"Girl you think you're coming with me to fight and you're already bruised up?"

"And why not?" She asked, ready for war.

That was my bitch, always down regardless of what her own situation was; I loved her for that.

I paused for a second and then said, "Fuck it." I started the car and we were out.

"Where does she live at again Renee?"

"She lives in Fields Corner, off Bowdoin Street."

Renee folded down the passenger seat mirror and began analyzing her bruised grill. I frowned at the sight of her fucked up face. Renee was my girl, so when something happened to her, I felt like it was happening to me.

"Yo, when we done with Ashley we are driving right over to my brother Trè's block to kick it with his boys. One of them niggas are gonna have to get at Tank for putting his hands on you straight up."

She put her glasses back on and sat back.

"Hell yeah, that nigga lost his mind doing this shit."

Twenty minutes later we arrived on Bowdoin Street. The block wasn't that full, it was a little too chilly for niggas to be out anyway so it was perfect timing for us to handle

93

our business. Renee pointed at a green house. "That's her crib right there, number 120 and that's her sitting there braiding some niggas hair. I heard she be making money braiding the heads of some of the nigga's she be selling weed to."

I pulled over and parked a little further up from her house. We had a clear visual of Ms. muthafuckin' Ashley. I wanted to get out right then and there and mop the sidewalk with her whack ass weave. I felt like every other woman would feel if they came in contact with their man's mistress, I wanted to off her.

It wasn't too long until she twisted up the last braid and the dude stood up to pay her. I cracked my door anticipating for him to walk off so that I could catch Ashley before she went into her crib.

"T, chill out, wait till the nigga leave, you see my face, I ain't trying to fight no more dudes today." I ignored Renee and kept my eyes on Ashley and placed one foot on the curb. As soon as that dude sat in his car and peeled off, I ran up to the porch like a track star and snatched Ashley up by her hair. She was completely caught off guard.

She screamed, "Get the fuck off me!" When she peeped my face and realized it was me, a look of shock spread across her grill.

"Remember me bitch?" I asked before pounding the fuck out of her face. "Your nasty ass is still calling my man,

A Hood Chick's Story Part II

you just don't get enough you thirsty ass stank ass bitch!" I threw blows to her face and body. I was actually fighting over a damn man which was pissing me off even more. I tried to make excuses for it in my head. My biggest excuse being that Ashley was disrespecting my family so fuck fighting over a man, I was fighting for Shayonna.

Ashley began exchanging punches with me and tried to match up to my skills. She screamed out for her friend, "Kiaaa! Come out here."

Her friend heard her cries and rushed outside and flew down the stairs once she noticed us fighting. Renee immediately snatched her up and started handling her. I managed to gain full control of my fight with Ashley and had that ho on the ground. She began running her mouth more than I was.

"Bitch, you're just mad cause your man keeps coming back!"

I kicked her harder making sure that I would leave bruises on that mouthy bitch but she continued to pop off at the mouth.

She uncovered her face to let out some words that I'm sure she regretted moments later.

"That's why we fucked in your house, in your bed." She couldn't cover her face fast enough and I stomped her in the mouth as hard as I could. I made her eat them fuckin' words. I stomped hard enough to knock all of her teeth out but they were still intact however drowned in blood. The stomp also managed to shut her up. She covered her mouth and lay frozen in pain. That was enough for me, I felt like revenge was well served and she lay in excruciating pain.

I glanced over at Renee and even though I was all riled up from giving Ashley the business, I kinda giggled at the sight of Renee digging in Ashley's friend's ass with a baseball cap and glasses on. The sight of that shit was hilarious. I walked toward Renee to pull her crazy ass off of Ashley's friend because she was beating her like she was getting revenge on Tank; she was letting a lot of frustration out on that bitch.

When I looked down at the girl, I couldn't help but notice that she looked familiar, she kept blocking her face from Renee's kicks but I could tell that I knew her. When Renee finally stopped kicking her I realized that the girl was Takia. Boston seemed too damn small at that point.

Takia was a bitch that I had got into countless fights with growing up. We were arch enemies. I whooped her ass so many times that I was now beginning to think that Ashley tearing my family apart was karma for everything that I been through with punk ass Takia. At first I couldn't tell it was her because she got a bit chubby. I had heard through the streets that she had like two seeds from two different niggas. But damn, she truly let herself go and now looked a sloppy ass mess.

A Hood Chick's Story Part II

"Come on Renee let's go!" We jogged back to the car.

"You see who that was T?"

Renee was just as shocked as I was to see Takia. I peeled off and Renee continued talking pounding her fist into her palm.

"Dog, out of all the bitches in the world, her homegirl is Takia. I haven't seen that bitch in years. She got all big and shit. She's ugly as fuck now."

We both laughed.

"And T, I seen that stomp you dropped on Ashley's grill." She reached over to give me dap. "It's still in you my nigga. I thought the suburbs took the hood out of you."

I glared over at Renee. "Bitch please never that, I just ain't fighting over petty shit anymore. But when it comes to my family and friends, anything goes. You already know."

"I respect that, you one loyal bitch."

I continued to drive, my destination was now Trè's block which was about a ten to fifteen minute drive depending on which way I drove. I knew that there would be a few niggas outside that I could talk to about getting at Tank for Renee. It was a gamble by doing this because niggas would do anything for me on the strength of Trè but Renee had no older brothers or other niggas that would ride for her so I had to take charge of this. She was my homey so

97

I felt like I had to do something. Hopefully they would just shake Tank up or fuck him up enough to know not to ever put his hands on her again.

I decided to take the back streets to Trè's block which led me to roll by the apartment building where I grew up. The sight of the building was too painful for me to face. Renee noticed my eyes glossing up while rolling by the building and she sympathized by gently rubbing my back. All I kept picturing was me, my mom and my two brothers living in that building at a time when we were all happy. It brought back so many painful memories in my life that I often tried to block out in order to maintain my sanity that I had to look the other way.

My mom cutting me and Trè off and blaming us for the death of Sharod hurt like someone stuck a knife through my heart daily. We were supposed to be tighter than this. She was our mom, we were supposed to be each other's backbone and get through our loss together.

Instead, Trè and I only had each other as family and since he wasn't around I put my all into Tony and Shayonna. And look where the fuck putting my all into Tony is getting me?

I began to resent the hood. Don't get me wrong, it made me the strong individual that I am today but I felt like the dark cloud that has brought me bad luck since my youthful years was not only over my head but

A Hood Chick's Story Part II

overshadowing the whole hood. It was like a cloud of pure evilness. It caused many mothers to lose their children to the streets, bad choices and wrong decisions leaving a lot of hearts desolate.

I passed about four poles on the same block full of colorful teddy bears and "I Miss You" signs from the loved ones of people who lost their family or friends on that particular part of the street. I beeped at some of the drug dealers that I knew who were still hanging out on the same corners that they had considered their territory from back when I lived around there. I couldn't believe how some of them were still out risking their freedom nickel and diming. Some things just never seemed to change. But some people just have no way out so I did have to thank God for getting me out of the hood, even though I still had problems like the bullshit I was going through with Tony but I'll manage to brave it out.

The hood had changed so much since I lived around there.

There were new houses being built in spaces that were once empty lots where niggas used to stash burners at back in the day. New schools and church's being built, and they were even re-doing some of the projects. But the aura in the hood felt exactly the same.

"Tiaraaa O-OOO!"

LaShonda DeVaughn

Trè's friend Ken-Ken flagged down my car once I hit their block. I pulled up to the curb and Renee and I got out of the car.

"What's hood with y'all?" he hollered out.

"Nothing, we chillin'," I said.

"Word. What up with Trè, he maintaining?"

"Yeah he's chilling, I'll tell him you said what up."

"Yeah do that," Ken-Ken said.

I looked back at Renee and then back in Ken-Ken's direction.

"Listen Ken-Ken I have to holla at you about something." He switched to serious mode and he rubbed his hands together ready to hear what I needed.

His dusty wave cap under his blue fitted B hat and his oversized champion hoodie and busted Adidas sneakers had me under the impression that he was still one of the goons from Trè's block. Therefore he was the perfect person for me to talk to.

"Do you know a nigga named Tank?"

"Yeah I know that scram, he's from the projects around your old way."

"Come here Renee." I signaled and she walked closer to me and Ken-Ken and took off her glasses.

"Dammmmn!" Ken-Ken said with his eyes bucked. Renee quickly put her glasses back on and stepped back.

"So that nigga Tank did that?" Ken-Ken asked.

100

A Hood Chick's Story Part II

"Yeah he put his hands on her like a little bitch, I don't want you doing nothing crazy though just shake him up a little bit, put some fear in the nigga."

"Say no more, I got y'all." He had a serious expression on his face so I knew that he would handle Tank for me. He grabbed my shoulder and we began walking up the street leaving Renee standing by the car. He lowered his tone so that she couldn't hear him.

"Now T, I'm only doing this because you're my niggas peoples, your girl is cool and all but shit, hook a nigga up. Beefin' with Tank is gonna bring heat to the block so at least let a nigga get something out of it."

"Okay Ken-Ken I will talk to her for you, but I don't know about all that hook-up shit."

I chuckled inside at Ken-Ken being a typical dude trying to get something out of helping a chick.

"A'ight," he said as we stopped walking.

"Oh yeah Tiara, you throwing a bash for Sharod this year right?"

"Yeah, that's every year."

"A'ight, I know it's coming up soon too, you know we're gonna be there."

"That's what's up, I'll let ya'll know what spot I'm throwing it at a'ight?"

"A'ight."

101

LaShonda DeVaughn

He gave me a hug and then pulled out twenty dollars to put toward Trè's canteen. One thing about goonies, or niggas in the hood that are always going to war with other blocks was that it was hard for them to make money. They had too many enemies and couldn't be on certain blocks without having drama because they had to watch their backs too much. So I took his little twenty bucks as a good gesture but it would've only lasted Trè a few days at best. He was used to my $300 every two weeks toward his canteen.

On the ride back to drop off Renee, she asked, "What did that nigga say about me?"

I smirked before answering.

"He told me he wanted a hook-up."

"With who?" she asked raising her eyebrows.

I chuckled. "With you girl."

"Puh-lease! Picture me flossing around with his dusty ass."

Renee had me cracking up ragging on Ken-Ken the entire way back to her crib.

When we approached the projects, coincidentally Tank and Bianca were cuddled up beside Renee's project building door. They were amongst a whole bunch of other niggas who were smoking weed and playing dice and just hanging outside like on any other typical night. Tank kept sliding Bianca kisses on her lips from time to time and Renee took off her glasses to get a better look. When Tank slipped Bianca the tongue and basically had a make out session right in front of us, Renee was heated.

"Ha! I wonder how I taste to Bianca's dumb ass."

She spoke as if she was proving a valid point but it was only her jealousy showing out loud.

"Bianca is a dumb ass bitch, she's fuckin' stupid. The nigga was fuckin' me today and her dumb ass is over there all over him. Chicks are so fucking blind, look at her over there smiling and shit like they have a perfect relationship. Only if she knew! Shit if I wanted to I could suck up to him and have him lickin' my twat all fuckin' night. She's lucky I hate that nigga right now."

I got lost in Renee's words. I had just beaten Ashley's ass for being exactly how Renee was, a sideline ho. And the way Renee was downing Bianca it was as if she was doing something wrong by being with her man. He was in fact, *her* man, not Renee's. She had every damn right to be all over *her* man. Renee looked in their direction with her face all balled up.

"I don't even want to walk past them, drop me off at my cousin Kathy's crib down the street T, I need to get my mind right."

Renee didn't say another word on the way to her cousin's house, the make out session had pissed her off to the point to make her speechless, and Renee was never speechless. She placed her head in her palm and rested her elbow against the car window and occasionally sucked her teeth. She was truly mad, mad and desperate because I wasn't expecting the dumb shit she asked before we approached her cousins crib. I pulled up and parked and Renee opened the door putting one foot outside.

"T, can you give Ken-Ken my number?"

"Huh?" I asked puzzled.

"Come on T, don't look at me like that, give him my number, he could just be a friend."

"Renee stop acting desperate and no I'm not giving him your number. You can't be serious right now. You act like you can't be without a dude or some shit. You were right, you do need to get your mind right because you're talking out ya ass. You were just clowning the nigga the whole ride back and all of a sudden you want to hook up with him?"

She was aggravated and didn't want to hear shit I had to say.

"Fuck it Tiara! Just forget it." She slammed my door and stormed into her cousin's crib.

I drove home and didn't even give Renee's bullshit a second thought. I had my own damn problems.

A Hood Chick's Story Part II

All the lights were out downstairs and the house was quiet so I assumed that Tony put the baby to bed. When I got upstairs Tony was on the phone and I could hear him yelling before I even reached the bedroom door. I knew that it had to be Shawn. They had the same cocky attitude and always seemed to clash when they go on the phone.

When I walked into our bedroom, I didn't acknowledge Tony as I normally would. I went inside our bedroom bathroom and ran the shower water after laying out my clean undergarments on top of my dresser. I didn't even tune into his conversation although from the tone of his voice it sounded very heated. I shut the bathroom door and peeled off my clothing and stepped into the hot shower.

I became paralyzed in relaxation closing my eyes and letting the water beam down on my body hitting all the right places to relax me. I opened my eyes intending to reach for the soap when I noticed inside our shower sliding door rail was a pair of turquoise lace panties hanging from it. All that relaxation shit went right down the drain with that water. I was pissed! At first I thought my mind was playing tricks on me. I picked up the panties with my fingertips because I wanted to check the size to make sure I wasn't bugging although I knew they weren't mine but my anger had my mind on some naive shit. I knew this nigga couldn't be this stupid and have a bitch in our crib while our daughter was home; I know he had to have that much respect for me.

I looked at the size of the panties and it read large. I was nowhere near a size large so this meant that he either had a fat bitch over our crib or a chick with a huge ass. I felt stupid as shit and was even more furious at the fact that I had just whooped Ashley's ass thinking that my mistress problem was over but he was still at it with another bitch in my damn house possibly on my damn bed!

My head spun in a few twirls and I almost tripped over my own foot trying to get out of the tub in a hurry. As I walked toward the door, I heard Tony's voice coming closer and closer toward me. It seemed as if he was walking up to the bathroom door on the other side simultaneously. At that point, everything went so fast, I don't know what the fuck happened. I opened the door with the panties hanging from my finger ready to blast on him and all I heard him say was "NOT MY 80G'S!"

That was the last thing I remembered. I blacked out on the bathroom floor.

A Hood Chick's Story Part II

I don't know if I got smacked or punched but bottom line, Tony knocked me the fuck out.

I woke up laid out in the middle of the bathroom floor; my head was throbbing in pain to the point where it hurt to open my eyes. I held my head with both hands trying to stop it from spinning.

I heard Tony in our bedroom on the phone yelling and screaming making my head hurt worse. He was throwing things around. I heard glass breaking and objects being thrown against the wall. He yelled through the phone, "Shawn, nigga tell me your fuckin' lying. I will kill that bitch!"

I was confused, I didn't know what Tony was raging about and more importantly why he put his hands on me. I managed to stumble out of the bathroom into our bedroom trying to muster up the strength to confront him. I looked around for something hard because I was going to bust him over the head with something. I had never got laid out before in my life and I really didn't give a fuck about what he was raging about because whatever it was shouldn't have caused him to lose his damn mind and hit me like I was a fuckin' man. I snatched one of our lamp cords out of the wall and began walking toward him with intentions on busting the lamp over his hard ass head.

When he turned and saw me, he folded his phone closed hanging up on Shawn without saying goodbye and

107

LaShonda DeVaughn

rushed toward me. I was shook! He charged over toward me like a hockey player on blades knocking the lamp out of my hand and forcing me to the wall by my arms.

"Tiara what did you do! What the fuck did you do!"

I've never seen Tony in that state, his eyes were bloodshot red and it was as if he had no control over himself, needless to say, I was scared. I had no idea what was going on.

"What are you talking about Tony! Let me go! Get off of me, now!" I pleaded while looking down at the lamp that I still intended to bust him over the head with.

He released me and turned as if he had lost a fight. He sat on the bed powerless placing both hands on his head. I picked up the lamp walking toward him. "Tony, what the fuck is going on? Why the fuck did you hit me like that? You're going crazy!" I was crying and my head was throbbing excessively.

I was so hurt that he had actually hurt me like that but as much as I wanted to retaliate, I couldn't bring myself to bust the lamp over his head.

He looked up and yelled, "My money, my fucking money is gone!" He stood and snatched the lamp out of my hand and sat me on the bed holding my arms and looking at me. "My money T, that shit is gone!"

108

A Hood Chick's Story Part II

I was still confused. "What are you talking about Tony, what money, what the fuck is going on, why are you doing this?"

His eyes were filled with tears but I could tell they were tears of anger.

"Did you and one of your girls go to Ashley's house today?"

I played dumb. "What are you talking about?"

"Answer me Tiara, this ain't the time to act stupid, did you and somebody go over to Ashley's house and fight her?"

I looked at him without answering wondering what me fighting Ashley had to do with anything and I could tell he was getting impatient.

"Tiara, I'm gonna ask you one more time, I know that stupid bitch Renee probably talked you into it because you left that hoodrat shit behind. Was it her? Did you go over there with Renee?"

I stood to my feet. "Yes I did and no Renee didn't convince me to go over there; I went over there because you were still messing with that bitch so I took matters into my own hands to make that ho stay away from my family."

Tony was pissed! He turned around and began punching the air and then he stopped and spoke angrily through his teeth.

"Well Tiara you just fucked up our family. That bitch had 80 G's of mine and 20G's of Shawn's money. She was going to Miami to cop us some weight and bring that shit back."

Now I was really confused. "Why would you give her all that money to risk Tony? You run a successful business, why are you dipping back into this drug shit?"

"Listen!" he shouted cutting me off. "I had this shit planned perfectly. She was gonna meet my connect, cop the weight and drive it back in a U-haul truck that her grandmother rented. It was gonna take them 24 hours to get there, one day to finish the transaction and 24 hours to get back. Now I get this phone call from Shawn telling me that she called him telling him that you and some chick came to her crib disrespecting her house and now that bitch disappeared and is nowhere to be found with our money."

Tony sat back on the bed and took my arm forcing me to sit with him. "Tiara, I'm so sorry for hitting you, I swear on my life I didn't mean to hit you the way I did in the bathroom. When I heard that she left with my money because of you, I reacted out of anger."

I couldn't sympathize with him, fuck that, he hit me over some side dealings that I had no idea about, my mode was in total "fuck him" state, he fucked up with me. So, I dug for more answers because none of this made sense to me.

A Hood Chick's Story Part II

"Tony, I still don't understand why you would risk that money when you have a successful firm."

"You're starting to piss me off asking all this irrelevant shit."

"What the fuck are you talking about Tony, its VERY fuckin' relevant."

"Okay Tiara, let me break it down for you. I couldn't tell you that I was dealing with Ashley on the side for business because I didn't want to hear your mouth but I was not fucking her. I was just using her for money purposes. You're so worried about me fuckin' her and all I was worried about was getting money. When she called my phone earlier, she just wanted to set up a time to meet me to go over everything before me and Shawn gave her the money. I left work today and met up with her and one of her friends in the bank parking lot and we gave them the money."

I interrupted. "Wait, what was her friend's name?"

"Here you go asking irrelevant shit again."

"Tony, I'm serious what is her friend's name?" I was hoping I didn't already know the answer to this question.

"I don't know, Kia, Takia or some shit. We checked her out, we know where she lives and the whole nine. What does it matter what her name is?"

"Nothing," I said letting him finish talking. I couldn't tell him that his money was left in the hands of my

111

old enemy. Now that she knew that it was my man whose money that she was holding, the outcome was bound to turn out bad.

"Both of these bitches are hoodrats so two hoodrats cant' get too far with that money. Man Tiara, if these bitches really disappeared with my shit, I will go to Ashley's crib and tie up her whole family if I had to." He calmed down and put his hands on my face causing me to cringe from the hit.

"I'm so sorry Tiara, I am. I apologize a million times for hitting you. I also apologize for making these moves behind your back but I couldn't tell you about the business. I didn't know how.

"What do you mean you couldn't tell me about the business? The firm is definitely successful Tony. Of all people, I know that. I mail all the checks off and pay everything on time, I'm in charge of the firm's accounting if you want to get technical with it."

He started fidgeting and looked agitated.

"What's the problem Tony, spit it out." I said.

"Okay, look," he started. "I have been stopping payments on all of the checks that you've been sending off. The business is going bankrupt. The market has been dead because the recession is still affecting the economy, you know that. The petty accounts that we have aren't going to keep the business afloat. So I did some side shit, scams and what have you, but they all flopped. That's why I tried to do what I knew best, cop some weight and keep us elevated before you found out."

I sat dazed. I tried to digest the word "bankrupt" but it was a tough pill to swallow. Now I knew why Susan and I couldn't figure out why the numbers in the accounting books weren't adding up. Susan was smart, she caught it immediately but I just figured that either the system had a glitch in it or that some of the numbers were written incorrectly. But all the while it was Tony who had fucked up our calculations.

"See baby look at you, this is why I couldn't tell you, this is the reason why I tried to make moves first. I didn't want to see you looking like that. So now you know why I've been stressed."

"So, so what does all this mean Tony? Does this mean that we could lose everything and you weren't gonna tell me?"

"Nah baby, I told you, I was going to tell you but I didn't know it would be like this. Once I flipped that weight, I was gonna try and sell off the company before we lose it if it's not too late and start off fresh doing something else. Maybe a barber shop, rental car company in the hood or something. I wasn't gonna keep hustling and risking my freedom. I know I'm on parole. But I'll tell you this much and I mean it with every bone in my body." He pounded his fist on his own chest. "The only way that I would go back to jail and risk losing you and Shayonna is if this bitch doesn't come back with my money. I will die before I go broke."

Tony's cell phone rung and he hopped off the bed to grab it off the dresser.

"Shawn what's up, you hear anything?"

While Tony continued his conversation with Shawn, I felt my face throbbing and I got up to check it out in the bathroom mirror. I discovered that my right eye looked identical to Renee's. It wasn't sealed shut, but the corner of it was swollen and turning a disturbing purplish blue color. I was heated. What kind of life was I living? I had chosen the wrong man. He had made these hot ass decisions without my knowledge, not me, and I didn't deserve to be hit. Furthermore, the fucking business was going bankrupt?!

The only thing that made me content at that moment was the fact that I would be closing on some property that I could afford without needing Tony. If we lose the business, my property would bring me in enough income for Shayonna and me to live comfortably.

I thought a bit deeper into the situation generalizing the play of events that just took place and Ashley and Tony were the common denominators. Yeah Tony had fucked up and although he had done most of the work providing us with the lifestyle that my daughter and I were now accustomed to living, I felt like I deserved every piece of it

A Hood Chick's Story Part II

and no broke down hoodrat bitches was gonna come and snatch the rug from under my feet. So yeah he may have fucked up with his dumb ass judgment calls but I was still a rider and Ashley and Takia would not be victorious in playing a part of my family being broke so it was on.

I walked back into the bedroom and heard Tony tell Shawn to "suit up" and that he was on his way. I ran to the closet and threw on my Lacoste jogging suit and scrambled through my shoes to find my Gazelle Adidas to match. I rushed it all on and stopped Tony before he headed out.

"Wait Tony, I'm coming. Call your aunt and tell her that we are bringing the baby over."

"You're coming where?" He asked.

I looked at him with all seriousness. "To get at them chicks, I'm down for whatever y'all are planning right now."

He shook his head. "I know you're playing right? What I look like bringing you with us to handle some hot shit like this? You don't need to be out here, stay here and take care of my daughter. I'm handling this, I fucked up so I'm gonna fix it."

I pointed to my eye. "You see this? Do you realize all of the bullshit that I have been going through lately has been over Ashley? Do you know how stressed I have been at how she has basically destroyed my family, the only solid family that I have left? Tony I should have been left you and you know it. You cheated and started putting your hands on

115

me on a regular and Ashley has been the reason. So yeah, I'm going."

With those last words, Tony stepped aside and allowed me to walk in the hall and he followed behind me. He had no choice but to respect my words. He knew that I was right. Plus the loyalty in me couldn't leave him broke, I just couldn't let these chicks win.

I threw some clothes on Shayonna and met Tony at his car.

"My aunt said we could bring her over," Tony said as Shayonna and I were seated.

Tony's appearance was much more calm nonetheless I could tell he was still heated. He had on his black Champion hoodie, which I hadn't seen him wear in years. He had on some black denim jeans and black Timberland boots. It was clear that his focus right now was on getting his money and he was dead serious about it. Mine on the other hand was on getting the money and getting at Ashley and Takia for thinking that they really fucked me up by disappearing with my family's money. I was using this time to get at them in the worse way and this was the perfect time to do it.

A Hood Chick's Story Part II

Chapter Eight – The Mission

We dropped off the baby to Tony's aunt and then picked up Shawn. He walked by the passenger side grilling me before entering the car.

"What the fuck happened to your eye?" he asked.

I had forgot that my eye was swollen because my adrenaline had taken over, I just wanted to hurry up and get this over with.

Suddenly, reality sunk in as I realized that this was one of those situations that I had fought so hard to put behind me. I was a mom now; I was supposed to be home with my daughter enjoying life. I guess you could say that I was reaping the benefits of being with a dope boy that couldn't help but dip back and forth into the hustling life not thinking of how it would affect his family. But like I said, I just wanted to get this over with.

"Fuck all that," Tony said referencing to Shawn to mind his business regarding my eye. "Just tell me where we're going."

"A'ight, I found out that them hoes are at the Holiday Inn in Dedham. But we have to stop at Easy's crib first to pick up some burners."

Tony turned quickly to look at Shawn in the back seat.

"What the fuck happened to the two hammers I gave you to hold?"

"Dog, I told you my little cousins and them used them burners. They probably got body's on them so I sold them."

Tony was pissed. "Nah nigga you didn't tell me that shit! So where the fuck is my money for them if you sold my shit?"

"Your money?" Shawn asked dumfounded.

"Yeah nigga, you just said you sold my burners, so where the fuck is the money from the sale?"

"Oh, oh, I got you. Matter fact, I'll buy the two we getting from Easy."

Tony mean mugged Shawn and we sat in silence for a few seconds.

"You lucky you my nigga cause that's some cornball shit you did." Tony shifted in his seat and started talking shit while starting the car.

"I can't believe this nigga sold my two hammers and didn't fuckin' tell me." He peeked at Shawn through the rear view mirror and continued barking on him as we left the parking space.

"Nigga I only asked you to hold my hammers because I don't like keeping them hot shits in the crib with my girl and my daughter."

"A'ight dog." Shawn blurted out aggravated that Tony was still rambling on. "I said I got you."

We made our way to Easy's crib and Shawn went inside and copped two burners. One was a .38 like the two that Tony had Shawn hold for him and the other one was a nickel plated 9mm. I was familiar with all types of guns since my teenage years. My brother Trè always showed me different calibers of guns when he would cop them and him and I would curiously play with them.

While heading to the hotel, Tony went on and on about how I needed to apply for my gun permit so that we could have a gun in the house legally. Since my assistant Susan's father was a police officer I had already inquired about the steps to apply for my gun permit and she told me that she would find out.

Once we arrived at the Holiday Inn, we parked the car in a dark corner under an overshadowing tree. We were out of the view of cameras and hopefully of witnesses. Thankfully the lot wasn't that full and we had a good view of the U-haul truck once we spotted it. We sat for a while before we went in because we had to strategize. Tony lit his blunt and took a few long puffs before passing it to Shawn. For as long as I've known Tony, he had smoked weed like they were cigarettes. He smoked when he woke up, when he took his morning shit, and he even smoked a few times while we fucked. And he was so cocky about his habit that if you asked him about it, he would tell you that he only smoked that good shit. He smoked so much I don't even think that he got high anymore. His eyes wouldn't get chinky and he maintained his normal composure so no one at work could ever tell the difference. It didn't seem to affect his memory neither, Tony was so good with numbers that he could do them in his sleep. I guess that's due to his long history of hustling. Thinking back on when Tony taught me how to cook, cut and weigh drugs doesn't really tickle my fancy. Each time my measurements were off, whether it were measuring grams of coke or weed, Tony would go over what I done and point out how much I was off so that I'll get it right. I respected it though; he was risking his life every time he served a play so he wanted his money right.

"A'ight Tiara, I want you to go get the room number and shit at the front desk. Me and Shawn are going to slide through on the low and meet you at the elevators."

Tony took in a few more puffs and then exhaled. "Shizz, they might have some niggas up there so make sure you got the toast in good reach. Don't do nothing stupid to make us hot neither."

A Hood Chick's Story Part II

I nodded, agreeing with Tony. I hated when niggas got nervous and did dumb shit. I didn't want no mistakes because I had a lot to lose. Shawn was definitely that crash dummy type nigga. He was cocky like Tony but sometimes he was too cocky. The type of nigga that would test you and then bow down when he met his match.

For instance, Tony had told me this story of how he rode with Shawn one day to serve one of his plays. Shawn went in the house to serve the dude but dude short changed him and told him that he'll hit him with the rest of the money the next day. Shawn told the dude that the next day wasn't good enough but dude told him that his word was bond. Shawn stormed out of the dudes crib and went to go get Tony who was waiting for him in the car. He banged on the car window and when Tony rolled down his window, Shawn was being obnoxiously dramatic going on about how the dude short changed him and he added mad gas to the story saying that the dude told him he ain't giving his money as if dude was trying to play him. He got Tony all fired up and Tony went back inside with Shawn to confront dude. Tony approached dude, who was one of his previous customers from when he was in the game, and dude told him the truth; that he told Shawn that he'd pay him the next day.

Tony was cocky about the situation. He took the upper hand and asked dude why he was trying to get gutter with Shawn by telling him he wasn't giving him his dough.

121

LaShonda DeVaughn

The dude looked at both of them like they were crazy and asked Shawn why the hell he made up some bullshit to tell Tony. That's when dude got gully with Shawn and stepped to him on some drama shit.

Dude was a goonie too. Tony said he'd never seen fear in Shawn's eyes like he did that day. He said Shawn couldn't even look dude in his eyes when he stepped to him. Like I said, the dude was one of Tony's previous customers so Tony knew he was good for the money because he used to let him slide and pay him a little later when he dealt with him. He didn't understand why dude would get gully with Shawn about paying him but when dude told him the truth, Tony knew Shawn added shit to the story. Shawn was trying to get his money right then and there and he thought by bringing Tony in to confront dude with him that would force the dude to scrape up the cash and bitch out. He had another thing coming. Tony separated them and told dude that they'd come to collect the next day and that was that. Shawn could have also handled that situation that simple but he had to try to be tough.

And that's the type of nigga Shawn was, just tough for no reason. In my opinion, I call dudes like that cornballs or like 50 Cent would say, a wanksta. But he was Tony's homeboy and that's the only reason I entertained his presence.

122

A Hood Chick's Story Part II

Our plan was now executed so all I had to do was get the hotel room number. I went through the hotel double doors and entered the lobby. I approached an elderly hotel clerk who was actually falling asleep while sitting in the stool at the front desk.

"Excuse me."

My greeting woke him up immediately and I cracked a smile.

"How are you?" I asked. "My name is Latrice Henderson and I'm looking for my sister Takia Henderson and my cousin Ashley.

The old guy disregarded me and focused directly on my face. "Are you okay young lady, your face is bruised pretty badly?"

I grabbed my shades out of my purse and slid them on. "I'm okay sir thanks for asking, can you tell me what room my sister Takia Henderson is in?"

The old man took his attention off of me and searched through the reservations. "Well let's see." He squint his eyes at the screen. "I don't see anyone with the last name Henderson. Do you know what Ashley's last name is?" I hesitated because I didn't know it but I remembered Takia's last name was Henderson from back in the day so I had hoped that the room was reserved under Takia's name.

A few more seconds of searching, he located the reservation.

LaShonda DeVaughn

"Oh here we go, Takia Henderson," he said. "That would be room 207."

"Room 207?" I repeated and smiled.

"Thank you very much sir, you enjoy your night."

I headed for the elevators. Tony and Shawn had already made their way there however Shawn suggested that we take the stairs since the elevators most likely had cameras in them. We just wanted to avoid being hot by all costs. We walked up two flights and then down the long carpeted hotel hallway before we spotted room 207.

I knocked on the door. I had to knock a few good times before they turned down the music. I heard them whispering. "Shh! Shh!" Someone asked, "Who is it?" It was Takia's voice.

I replied, "Room service."

Her dumb ass didn't even try to look out the peek hole although I was standing out of its view. She just opened the door and as soon as she did Tony and Shawn burst in and I followed.

"What the fuck is this?" Takia screamed out before bolting toward Ashley on the bed nearest to the back of the room.

We scanned the room to see if they had any niggas with them but it was only the two of them. I could tell Takia was scared to death and didn't know what to expect. I read the same fear in both of their eyes. I stood by the door and made sure there was nowhere for them to try to run. The looks on their faces were as if they'd seen a ghost. They weren't expecting this. On the other bed there were a bunch of clear stuffed freezer size bags full of weed. It looked to be about twelve or so packs.

I saw money scattered over the dresser and big bags of clothes from AJ Wright. These dumb bitches didn't even know how to shop. If you were going to risk your life and steal a hundred G's from drug dealers at least buy luxury shit like Gucci or Louis Vuitton. I saw Baby Phat and Rocawear tags pulled off near the trash barrel. I chuckled at how dumb these chicks were. Tony and Shawn stood over the duo as they were sitting on the bed crying and staring at the floor.

"Where's my money!" Tony yelled. They were shivering and crying pretty loudly. Shawn took his gun out of the back of his pants and cocked it.

"We gon' ask y'all bitches one more time, where the fuck is our money?" They began crying even louder and Tony pulled out his gun and told me to turn up the music. I knew that he wasn't going to shoot them but it sure scared them enough to want to finally begin to talk. I turned up the music and Tony cocked his gun.

"Okay, Okay!" Ashley said. "It's right there."

LaShonda DeVaughn

She pointed to the money scattered over the dresser. It appeared to only have a small amount of money, ten G's at the most.

"Bitch is that a joke?" Tony asked as he glanced over at the dresser. Shawn turned his gun around and pistol whipped Takia in the face forcing her body to lie back on the bed. Her nose was now leaking with blood and Ashley screamed.

"Ahhhh! What the fuck are y'all doing?" She leaned over to examine Takia's face.

"Bitch you're next if you don't show me where my fuckin' money is," Shawn demanded.

Ashley quickly stood up and knelt down and opened up a duffle bag full of money.

"Here! Take it, this is it."

Tony kicked the bag. "Bitch that ain't all of it!"

"That's all that's left." Ashley cried.

"Fuck you mean all that's left?" He rushed toward her. "Y'all bitches were out spending my fucking money?" Tony asked turning up his lips.

Ashley was scared shitless.

"Go sit on the bed," Tony demanded. He kicked the open duffle bag closer to the dresser and extended his arm over all of the money on the dresser and swiped it into the duffle bag. Ashley was on the bed with Takia comforting her as she continued to cry in pain from being pistol whipped.

A Hood Chick's Story Part II

Shawn was standing over them with his gun at his side with an evil smirk on his face; he was loving every minute of this, feeling like he was in control. He looked at the weed on the other bed and started toward it.

"I know y'all hoes didn't spend my fuckin' money on this weed. What y'all bitches thought y'all was gonna flip this shit with my money and come up?"

"No!" Ashley said shaking her head.

She looked as if she was trying to come up with some kind of explanation but there was nothing she could say to get them out of the mess they made.

"We bought that weed for y'all, we were gonna come bring it to y'all instead of going to Miami because we found a connect up here. Y'all really thought we were gonna take your money?" She tried to plead with Tony, "You know me better than that Tony; you know that I wouldn't do that to you."

She tried giving Tony that puppy dog look but that shit didn't work. He wanted to crack that bitch in the fucking head just as much as I did. And she only made me mad by trying to lure him in with that innocent shit. I wanted to stomp a mud hole in her ass again. Her face was already fucked up from our fight earlier and I had no problem with adding to it.

"What the fuck is this?" Shawn asked while picking up the bags of clothes from AJ Wright. He emptied them out unto the bed. Tons of clothes, socks, panties and bras tumbled out. There were even bags of baby clothes that Takia must've splurged on for her kids. Shawn laughed and turned back at Ashley and Takia.

"Shopping sprees and shit with my money huh?" He picked up some of the clothes with the tip of his gun and then took it and pistol whipped Takia in the face again just as she was about to sit up.

"What the fuck Shawn, stop, please!" Ashley cried as she watched Takia suffering.

"A'ight Shizz chill!" Tony said.

Shawn had his lips frowned up like he wanted to hit her again.

Takia and Ashley climbed all the way to the back of the bed with their backs against the wall so that they were out of Shawn's reach. Tony began searching through everything looking for more money. He went through all of the drawers, he flipped the mattress on the other bed and any money or weed that he found, he stuffed it into the duffle bag.

After thoroughly searching everything and not feeling like he found enough of his money he charged over at Ashley in frustration. He knelt on the bed and grabbed her by her neck. He was squeezing her neck so tight that she couldn't speak. I saw veins popping out of her forehead and

A Hood Chick's Story Part II

he spoke through his teeth. "Bitch where the fuck is the rest of my fuckin' money?"

Ashley tugged on his forearm with both hands trying to take his arm away from her neck so that she could speak but Tony squeezed harder and her brown skin was now beginning to redden.

"Let her go, you're going to kill her," Takia said panicked.

He finally let her go just in time, any longer, I'm sure she would have passed out. She coughed and held her neck with both hands. She was gasping for air and breathing heavily.

"We bought those clothes, this room, and that weed." Ashley said after regaining her breath.

Tony smacked her across the face and I cracked a smile. Shit, it made me feel good inside. This was his so-called mistress that stole from him so I knew for sure that this was the end of their little rendezvous. She held her face looking at Tony like she was shocked that he put his hands on her.

He yelled out for Takia to stand up next to Ashley.

"You heard him, stand the fuck up!" Shawn shouted.

"What?" Takia cried, "Look at my face, I'm bleeding."

Shawn grabbed her by her arm and yanked her up. "Bitch we don't give a fuck about your face, get the fuck up!"

They stood side by side holding each other.

"Strip!" Tony demanded.

"Strip?" Ashley asked.

Shawn put his gun in Ashley's face. "Bitch you heard him. Strip, take off your motherfuckin' clothes right now."

"A'ight Shizz back up," Tony said forcing him out of Ashley's face.

Takia cried in pain. "My nose is bleeding, I have to keep my head back, I can't strip. I don't have anything on me, y'all can search me."

Shawn ripped Takia's button up shirt open and told her to shut the fuck up and strip. She cried and started peeling off all of her clothes. They were both pulling off each piece of clothing slowly. I bent to sit on the other bed watching with a grin on my face. I felt like I was getting sweet revenge and I didn't even have to get my hands dirty. I enjoyed my man becoming his mistresses enemy, in a way, they both deserved to feel pain after putting me and my daughter through the bullshit that I went through over his cheating. I guess this was karma on both of their parts.

Shawn picked up their jeans and pulled out balls of money that were stuffed inside of their pockets.

A Hood Chick's Story Part II

"That's all of it I swear!" Ashley cried as she watched Shawn take the money from her jeans.

"Y'all must think this is a game." Shawn said.

"I thought you didn't have anything on you, so what the fuck is this?" He put the crinkled hundred dollar bills in Ashley's face.

Takia was covering her titties and pussy with her hands because she was stripped down to nothing at this point.

"That's *my* money, I already had that," Ashley said trying to explain.

"You like lying huh?" He lifted his gun to hit her again but Tony stopped him. "Dog, that's enough, let's be out."

All of a sudden, we heard the door.

Knock, Knock, Knock! A males voice hollered out. "Yo, open the door!"

Tony yanked Ashley by her arm and whispered, "Who the fuck is that?"

"It's my brother," she replied.

He pushed her toward the door and whispered, "Make him leave."

She turned the music down and as she got closer to the door Shawn whispered, "Ashley." She turned around to look at Shawn, he grabbed Takia and pointed his gun at her head, "Don't do nothing stupid."

131

Ashley nodded and proceeded to answer the door. I stood behind a wall out of the view of the doorway.

Ashley slightly opened the door.

"Damn what the fuck took you so long to get the door?"

Her brother tried to barge in but she only had the door cracked open enough to see his face.

"Wait, we ain't dressed," she told him as he tried again to push his way in.

"Well, throw something on," he demanded.

"Nah, go get us something to eat real quick, we'll need about thirty minutes."

"Hell no, I ain't going nowhere, throw something on and get dressed in the bathroom, shit."

"Bro, the food spot is next door, come on just go grab us something real quick."

Shawn, Tony and me were all looking at each other in the room, if her brother came in the room, we would have to handle him accordingly so we were ready for whatever.

Finally he let up. "Damn Ash, a'ight, y'all need to hurry up, give me the money, what y'all want?"

Tony walked up to the back of the door and handed Ashley a twenty dollar bill to give to her brother so that he could hurry up and leave.

She took the money on the low and then handed it to her brother.

A Hood Chick's Story Part II

"Here, just grab us some pizza or something a'ight."

"A'ight, I'll be right back," he said leaving.

It seemed as if we all exhaled. It literally felt like that shit was never going to end, we just needed to get out of this hotel and back to our spot to count the money.

Ashley closed the door and walked back toward us.

"Alright he's gone, could y'all please leave!" She sat on the bed next to Takia and they were both putting their clothes back on.

Shawn tried to sneak some pinches on Takia's nipples before she put on her bra.

"Stop," she shouted pushing Shawn's hands away but he just laughed it off; this was all fun to him.

Tony grabbed the large duffle bag and I began putting some of the clothes back into the AJ Wright bags because I was taking them. As I was putting the last of the clothes into the bags I laughed.

"Takia, you're still a dumb ass bitch huh? You thought you had me but the jokes on you bitch, jokes on both of y'all chickenheads. I'm taking these clothes with me, no ho will ever come up off me, remember that."

Tony and Shawn were already at the door waiting for me to hurry up. As I was heading out, I heard one of them mumble, "That's why you lost your brother bitch."

LaShonda DeVaughn

At that point, I lost control of myself, Shawn was in front of me and I yanked his gun out the back of his shirt and turned around and pointed it in their direction.

"Aaaaaaaaaaaaaaah!!!!" They both screamed in unison.

I didn't shoot, but I wanted to. I stood with my face tensed up pointing the gun. I felt so disrespected at the comment they made about my little brother Sharod, I wanted to harm them both badly, but I had too much to lose. I wasn't stupid enough to shoot them.

The fear in their eyes was good enough for me, they were scared shitless and they should have been. Only a heartless bitch would say something so hurtful. They both jumped off the bed and laid on the floor scared I was going to shoot but Tony yanked the gun from my hand and we ran out of the room and left the hotel through the back entrance bolting to the car.

"What the fuck Tiara, you fucking crazy!" Tony yelled pulling out the lot.

"Nah Tony, I feel her, I heard what that bitch said, that shit was straight disrespectful, I would have killed one of them bitch's if that were me," Shawn said from the backseat.

"Nah dog, ain't nobody killing nobody. Fuck what they say, their words ain't putting money in our pockets, you gotta be smart, do shit right."

134

A Hood Chick's Story Part II

It was just like Tony to think about money instead of the root of anything else. But I was just glad that we got his money and were now on our way back home.

During the ride, I felt stupid for having participated in something that was so unnecessary and furthermore it was over a mistake that Tony made. He should have told me about the business going bankrupt from the beginning and we could have tried doing something else to help out our family. He put his trust in a hoodrat bitch and now we were fucked up in the game. I had to fault myself for fighting Ashley earlier like I was still a damn teenager because I was too old for this shit. But there was something in me that I couldn't fight when I felt as though someone close to me is being wronged or that someone was wronging me. Some may call it loyalty but is it loyalty when I put myself in a predicament to fuck up *my* freedom? Is this a quality in myself that I should change? I thought about these questions the whole ride back to our crib, but only time would tell if it was in fact *me* that needed to change.

LaShonda DeVaughn

Chapter Nine – The Aftermath

We called and arranged for Tony's aunt to bring Shayonna to school for us in the morning and we arrived at our crib to count the money. Tony sat on the couch and poured all of the money out of the duffle bag onto the glass coffee table while Shawn sat beside him weighing up the freezer bags of weed.

"Crack this dutch for me Tiara!" Tony said while handing me a Dutch Master before he began his count. I cracked the seal open, split and emptied his blunt and handed it to him. It was a routine thing for me. I didn't know how to roll but it was second nature for me to crack Tony's Dutch Masters prepping them for him to roll.

After a frustrated Tony counted the money four or five times, he asked me to recount it to make sure he wasn't bugging.

"This is thirty G's," I said to Tony when I finished counting the money for the second time.

"Yeah that's the same shit I got," Tony said.

"Shawn, how much is that in weed." He asked.

A Hood Chick's Story Part II

Shawn put the last of the weed on the scale and then in frustration blurted out, "Dog first off this is some bunk shit; these dumb ass bitches could have at least copped some haze or some Kush. And they probably got overcharged for this. But nigga, this is only twelve G's in weed."

Tony sat back and inhaled his blunt but it wasn't enough to calm him. "I'll kill them bitches!" he hollered out punching the couch and startling me.

"That means them hoes spent most of my fuckin' money and altogether this is only fuckin' forty-two grand nigga?"

Tony was pissed! He wanted to harm someone or something bad.

He and Shawn sat on the couch circulating the blunt pissed off about their loss. All I could do was watch them. I thought they were the dumbest motherfuckers in the world to trust some hoodrat bitches with their money in the first place but then again what good girls would have agreed to do that shit?

"Dog, you're gonna have to take this 'L' Shawn, I gave them eighty G's nigga."

"What nigga? I ain't taking a complete loss. I ain't leaving here with nothing dog!"

Shawn was furious that Tony basically told him that he had to suck this up as a loss because he was keeping what was there. They continued to argue while I went into the half

137

bath downstairs to check on my eye. It had gotten bigger and I looked like I got fucked up by twenty people. I took my ass upstairs to get away from Tony and Shawn's arguing so that I could just sleep the rest of this stressful night away.

On my way upstairs, I thought about my life. I thought about Shayonna and the bond that she had with her father. Was I giving up on him at a time when he needed me the most? I didn't know what I wanted to do. If the business was going bankrupt and he just took this loss tonight, who could he fall back on? This is where I questioned my loyalty again. Thinking back, I was always loyal to people who didn't deserve it, now that I'm older, it seemed as if I was being taken advantage of. But being loyal was a part of being me; I was a real ass chick.

Yeah he cheated, hit me and disrespected me, but how real would I be to leave him stanking and by himself after he saved me from living a nightmare in the projects after my mom turned her back on me. Fuck what people thought about my situation, Tony needed me and until further notice, I was gonna be there for him.

As much as I just tried to absorb the fact that love had blinded me and tried to settle at being content with my situation, I quickly regained my sight in full force once I entered our upstairs bathroom and saw the turquoise panties still lying on the floor. I balled up my face disgusted and got an instant headache.

138

A Hood Chick's Story Part II

Fuck everything I just felt about being down for him; he fucked a bitch in our home! That was some unforgiveable shit.

I stormed out of the bathroom and had to walk over all of the broken shit on the floor in our bedroom to sit on my bed before I passed the fuck out. I had to sit for a good ten minutes to get my head right until I was finally able to contain myself. I massaged my own temples and took rapid deep breaths because my heart was fluttering immensely. I knew that this wasn't something I could let go or wait to talk about, I needed answers NOW; I could not let that shit ride.

True enough this probably wasn't the best time to bring it up because he was stressed about his money and the hot ass mission that we had just went on but fuck that, he had some explaining to do.

"Tonyyyy," I yelled out his name from the top of the stairs.

"What up!" he hollered back before appearing at the bottom of the stairs rolling yet another blunt.

"Come up here, we need to talk." I demanded.

"About what?" He crinkled his forehead not anticipating what I wanted to talk about because his stance was cocky; he knew that it wasn't something pleasant.
"Damn, here we go with some more bullshit." He paused, licked and sealed his blunt and waved me off. "A'ight yo I'll be up there in a second."

He was just about to go back into the living room with Shawn, but no sooner than he began to head that way, Shawn walked past him and without looking him in the face blurted, "Yo, I'm out." Shawn's tone was very nonchalant.

He was pissed of and I assumed that Tony must've given him little to no money for his cut from the money that they've lost. Shawn didn't give Tony no dap or nothing, he just opened the door and kept it moving. Tony turned to look at him and twisted his lips to the side to show he didn't give a fuck if Shawn was mad or not. He decided against going into the living room and proceeded to walk upstairs toward me.

As soon as he got up the stairs, I took the panties from behind my back and started cussing him out immediately.

"Who's are these?"

He took them out of my hand. "Fuck I'm supposed to know who's drawls these are?"

"The shit was hanging off the rail in the inside of our bedroom shower." I snatched them back and fingered for the label. "And look, the tag says 'Large'."

"Well if they were hanging off the shower in our bedroom then they are yours."

I was frustrated. "Do you see a size large over here Tony?" I pointed to my small ass. "Plus you would never catch me wearing this cheap ass lace. Now stop playing

140

A Hood Chick's Story Part II

dumb, what bitch did you have in here while I was gone, while my daughter was in here with you?"

Tony's usual cockiness emerged and he mean mugged me. "I know I'm not going through this shit right now Tiara. I'm tired of all this accusing me bullshit. You're really starting to aggravate me with this shit."

He headed toward our bedroom to diffuse the situation, he had hoped that I would just let it go but it only angered me more.

I stood there with my eyes bucked wide, I was actually being ignored so I was about to let this nigga have it.

How the fuck was I aggravating the nigga who's doing the fuckin' cheating? I played my part. He was the one coming up short.

"Oh so you're tired of it Tony!" I yelled. He kept walking and then slammed the bedroom door behind him. At this point I was truly enraged and fed up, I wanted to kill this dude. I envisioned Ashley's face in my head and who knows what bitch he done fucked in my house that left her shitty ass drawls that were now in my hands in my bathroom.

I threw them on my floor not caring where they landed. Whoever the bitch was most likely left them in my crib on purpose for me to find.

The stress started to hit me collectively and life was now once again confusing for me. Our company on the verge of bankruptcy, my fiancée putting his hands on me more than once and even worse than the beatings was the cheating. His cheating caused him to lose even more of the money that we needed. Fuck being loyal, he wasn't worth it!

I blanked out, I been through too much to be hitting a dead end again; I felt like insanity had overcome me. The room began spinning and I lost control of myself, I was vengeful and wanted to hurt Tony more than I ever had before. I stormed toward our bedroom and burst through the door and immediately charged at Tony. I was hitting him, kicking him, digging my nails into his skin and trying to make him hurt like I hurt.

"I hate you!!!!" I screamed while trying to fight this one hundred and seventy pound man. All it took was one forceful push by Tony and it landed me flat on my back on our bed, he rushed over and pinned me down. I was crying and screaming and just all together lost, I had nothing permanent in this world, my life was fucked up and I was convinced that it would never get better. "Get the fuck off of me, I hate you!"

He continued to pin me down as I tried to fight my way out.

"Tiara, how many times I have to keep telling you, you can't beat me." He kept pushing my body into the bed sinking me deeper into the mattress. "Stop doing this stupid shit or I'm gonna fuckin' leave you!" He hollered and squeezed me so tight, I was in so much pain, all I could do was spit in his face.

He stood up and then looked at me as if he was about to kill me. He wiped the spit with his hand and while doing so, I got off the bed and ran out of the bedroom. I ran so fast, I don't know if Tony tried to follow me to beat my ass for spitting on him or not but I was out. When I got downstairs, I took my keys and purse and I left. I cried hysterically while I was in my car. I had no destination and all I thought about was how much I've been deceived over the years by Tony. He couldn't have genuinely loved me. My own damn mother never even genuinely loved me. If it wasn't for Shayonna, I would probably be dead or in a crazy home.

Although I never received the love back that I deserved from people, I still loved hard. Loving Tony hard only came with a broken heart. I truly had to let him go. The plan that I had to leave him was actually always contemplated because something inside me always held me back and I felt like I would never be able to really do it. But I didn't have a choice, he wasn't good for me. I knew it would hurt me and Shayonna to our soul to depart from Tony but it was the best for us both. Tony was a problem and I had to cut him off. I cried and cringed at the thought of not being with the man whom I would lose my life for. I always thought that he was the only one whom kept my best interest at heart, but that was some bullshit.

Twenty minutes later, I found myself sneaking into the dark cemetery where my little brother was buried. It was closed but I needed to talk to him so I found a way in.

Now I know that cemeteries usually scared people, but to me, they were peaceful and harmless. I could never understand why people would be afraid of the dead when it was the living that posed a problem.

I walked through the damp mud finding my little brother's headstone only using the light from my cell phone. As soon as I located the stone, I sat in front of it.

"Hey Sharod." Tears stung my eyes as I spoke. "I need to talk to you." I took in a deep breath. "Every time I used to talk to you, you would listen giving me all of your attention, these days, I can't find anyone else that really cares about what I have to say." I frowned.

"Well I still haven't heard from Ma. I know you hear me saying that every time I come up here but I like to keep you updated in staying optimistic that one day she will reach out to me." I wiped the dirt off his picture on his head stone. "Man Sharod, why did you leave me here?" I cried. My tears fell onto his stone. "Why couldn't it have been me that was killed? You had so much more promised to you than I ever did." I sniffed. "You were so smart, so happy and confident. Me? Well go figure, my life hasn't gotten any better. The only one that I have in this world that loves me equally is Shayonna. She is getting so big Sharod, I wish you could see her, I talk about you to her all the time and she still kisses your picture every night." I forced a smile through my tears. "I just wish that you were here you know? I miss you Sharod, I just miss you." I stood there for a moment in silence before blowing a kiss to the picture on his stone and I walked off.

When I got home that night, Tony was sitting in the dark. He scared the shit out of me because I didn't see him sitting on the bed when I flicked on the light. I didn't know what to expect from him so I just stood there looking at him.

"T, man, I was sitting here thinking. I always apologize to you when I put my hands on you or when I feel like I wronged you. But looking back, you're a big part of a lot of our problems. I had to do three years in jail over you thinking that I was fuckin' a girl that had been out of the picture long before you and I met. You did that dumb shit you always do; fighting like it would always solve the problem. Now years later, you out here doing the same shit. You went fighting thinking that I was out here fuckin' around on you and I really wasn't. I never blamed you for shit T, but I never got an apology from you from things that you have done to put dents in our relationship."

I couldn't believe this motherfucker had the audacity to blame our problems on me. I never took his dick and stuck it in Ashley and I had no way of knowing that the bitch that snitched on him five years ago wasn't coming over to fuck him. He'd really outdone himself with this arrogant shit. He was king muthafuckin' cocky.

"Tony, I can't believe you're sitting here trying to piece together a puzzle that doesn't fit. That girl came to your house dressed to fuck five years ago and yeah I felt disrespected so I whooped her ass. No one told you to tell that ho where you lived, it wasn't my fault that she snitched on you. And let's not get on Ashley; you called me her name while fuckin' me Tony! You went behind my back for two years fuckin' the shit out of both of us and I never knew. So I bet if I was to find out who the bitch is that left her panties in our shower and fuck her up you would blame our problems on that too right?" I chuckled, "Man, fuck you Tony."

"T, man, I don't know what to say about us anymore straight up. We just went through all that bullshit today and I lost all that money and you were still on that dumb shit asking me about some damn panties?"

"You damn right! And if you can't understand where I'm coming from Tony then we really need to end it now."

"Fuck this!" He stood up. "All I know is that I gotta get this money. Fuck everything else man, I'm 'bout to be back on my grind. It's all about paper for me."

A Hood Chick's Story Part II

And with that said, Tony went downstairs to sleep on the couch and I slept in our bed stressed the fuck out. I could already feel that our relationship would never be the same.

LaShonda DeVaughn

Chapter Ten – Back In The Game

My eye healed just in time for my next hair appointment. I had become frequent with getting different weave hairstyles, I got hooked. This time my hairdresser put my shit in a hot ass 20-inch long weave ponytail and pushed my bang backwards at the top of my head into a stuffed hump. I had a black Paris Hilton type hairstyle and Tony loved it. He loved all the hairstyles I started getting. I kept switching my shit up to keep him on his toes but he was too worried about getting money to wonder what I was up to.

I devoted less time at the office since the business was sinking and I put more time and focus into my three family house since I had finally closed on the purchase. I couldn't help but pat myself on the back for obtaining a piece of property, a piece of the American Dream all by myself. Who would have thought a girl who struggled from the hood would gain the knowledge to obtain a great responsibility at such a young age? I had something to smile about again but even better, something that would stabilize me and my daughter's future.

A Hood Chick's Story Part II

I began acquiring numerous contractors to fix up things that needed repairing. There were a few kitchen cabinet doors that needed tightening and just minor plumbing problems, nothing major. I had a bunch of interviews with prospective tenants but found no one who fit the criteria of paying their rent on time during my screenings so the apartments would remain vacant until further notice.

I was also still successful at keeping my purchase a secret from Tony.

If I would have told him about it, he would probably ask me to set up drug operations out of the apartments instead of doing the right thing and getting tenants to give me clean money from rent. I couldn't risk my foundation, this was my ticket out, away from negativity and when I got enough money from it, away from him.

Tony on the other hand was heavily back in the game and everything was all about money to him once again. He was out at all times of the night reminding me of how things were when he was deep in the game back in the day. He would wear the same clothes for three or four days straight and not get a hair cut or line up for weeks. When he grinded, he *grinded* with no exceptions. Shayonna and I hardly saw him. He would come in, weigh his drugs, bag it up and leave out to serve the next play. I hated when he cooked up coke in my kitchen. It always fucked up my pots and forks because when the crack get's hard, it stuck to my

149

kitchenware like glue. What pissed me off the most was that he was doing that shit from our house knowing that my daughter lived there and that if we were to get raided, we would all go down and there would be a chance we could lose her. But things like that didn't bother Tony. He was ass backwards when it came to responsibility. All he saw in his world were dollar signs; me and Shayonna were just there and not even acknowledged as much anymore.

I tried to offer him different alternatives instead of staying in the game such as using his money to invest in some property or another business instead of using it on drugs. I stressed to him that we weren't those kids anymore back when we had no responsibility, we had a daughter now and being in the game wasn't a good look. Of course he was too cocky to take advice from me, he told me that he was done with the real estate shit and that he needed his money quick to re-coop for what he had lost. So I left it alone and let him do his thing.

I paid a hundred dollars for my gun permit and Susan hooked me up with the classes that I had to take in order to retrieve it. Once I completed the requirements and was approved for my license to carry, I copped myself a pretty little black 9mm. It was just for protection so I kept it locked up in a safe high in my closet far away from Shayonna. Shit, I even changed the lock on the safe so that Tony wouldn't figure it out. I didn't want him to try selling it to someone in the hood because I know plenty of niggas that used to get their burners from people with gun licenses and I wasn't trying to make myself hot.

Shawn's presence around my home dissolved quickly after the mission. Tony told me that he didn't give Shawn a dime of the money they took back from Takia and Ashley. So rightfully Shawn had a reason to be mad, however they shouldn't have done that stupid shit in the first place. But even Shayonna started asking about her "Uncle Shawn." He was her Godfather and he had taken a liking to my baby ever since she was born and she quickly grew attached. He used to drive Shayonna and me to see Tony sometimes when he was locked up when she was just a toddler. It was kinda weird not seeing him around as much as before but I didn't give a fuck, I never really liked him anyway.

It was early on a Saturday morning and Tony and I were heading to the office to clear out some of the stationary and hardware when I felt my phone vibrating through my purse.

"Hello," I answered.

"T, the ambulance, police and everything was just outside yo! They took Tank on a stretcher to the hospital," Renee spit out.

My heart was pounding in my chest and I was hoping that Ken-Ken and his boys hadn't killed him.

"Really? Is he straight?"

"Yeah I think he's straight, he got fucked up bad though and I think he got shot in the leg."

"Are you serious Renee?"

"Yeah girl, everyone is clearing out outside right now because they just took him away."

Tony was smoking a blunt while ear hustling and it apparently affected his driving because the police siren was flashing behind us and we were being pulled over.

"A'ight Renee keep me posted on that, I gotta go, I'll talk to you later." I quickly hung up the phone with Renee because I knew Tony was riding dirty.

"T, I got some crack in my ass but I need you to do something with this shit right here." He flashed me a few small bags of crack and I quickly stuffed them into my weave ponytail and a few of them in the hump on my head, my hairstyle had came in handy.

Tony put out his blunt and tried to spray some of his car freshener to drown out the weed smell and we waited for the officer to approach the car.

"License and registration please."

We already had the documents ready to give to the officer so that he could just write up a ticket and let us go.

He took the documents from Tony's hand, told him that he was speeding, then took a whiff of the odor and asked us to get out of the car. My heart was beating hard and fast.

A Hood Chick's Story Part II

The officer felt he had probable cause to search the car since the smell of Tony's hydro couldn't be flooded out by the air freshener.

"I smell marijuana in this vehicle." The officer said arrogantly.

"Well officer, we just picked up this car from my aunt, that smell must've been in there before we got the car," Tony lied.

The officer looked at him as if he was full of shit and began his search. He was determined to find something inside of Tony's car and Tony was nervous as shit. He was on parole and had no intentions on going back to jail. He completed three out of the five years he had to do in jail and would have to complete the last two years if he violated his parole in any way.

Tony stood tall trying to keep his composure and I was just as nervous standing on the curb beside him.

Back in Tony's hustle days, he had several cars with custom stashes inside for guns or drugs. But this wasn't back in the day and he was just jumping back in the game so shit was still a bit sloppy right now.

The police officer finished his non-thorough search and let us go with a warning. His prejudice ass was just mad that he didn't find any large quantities of drugs inside the car to convict us so he let us go.

153

LaShonda DeVaughn

There were a bunch of officers like that in the hood, they would let niggas go even if they had small bags of weed in their cars if they couldn't find anything harder in the cars to convict them with. But if you had money in your pockets, the officer would keep that shit and you would have to take that loss. Some say it's better than going to jail but no one wants to get got for their money like that.

When we drove off, I thanked God that the officer didn't thoroughly search our person individually and then thanked my angel Sharod for looking out for us. We definitely lucked up.

We still ended up doing some hot shit after getting pulled over. Tony got a phone call to serve two plays in Mission Hill. The plays were right across the street from each other. Tony asked if I could serve one so that we could hurry up. I used to be heavy into hustling with him but I didn't want to be hot and I only agreed so that we could hurry up.

I went into the crib to serve the fiend and when I walked out, this chick was on the porch grilling me hard. She was a young chick around seventeen or eighteen years old. She was looking at me like she wanted to shoot the ones with me. I didn't know if she was the little sister of someone that I had beef with or what but I was checking her early.

"You know me?" I said walking up on her.

154

A Hood Chick's Story Part II

Tony walked off the porch on the other side of the street and when he seen my face he yelled out, "Tiara, come on man, we don't have time for that shit."

"Nah you don't know me but I knew your little brother Sharod. I had a crush on him. And when I was younger me and my girls looked up to you and Ke-Ke and them."

She looked over at Tony's Beamer with admiration in her eyes. "I see you and T-Money are still doing y'all's thing. I respect it. Go and get your money little duffle bag girl."

I walked away, these little girls were looking up to me for all the wrong reasons. That one play that I served with Tony had this girl admiring the fact that I was with a drug dealer, shit had to change.

We got to the office and started clearing out things that we needed. I tearfully looked around displeased that our accomplishment was now about to be a simple memory. We hadn't even announced to the staff that the business was going under and I felt bad that we would be putting them out of a job. We gave it a good run but I guess all I could say is, shit happens. We planned to tell them on Monday that we would be closing the office the Friday following. We hadn't opened up any new accounts in weeks anyway and I made sure that I used a different lender when I made my purchase.

LaShonda DeVaughn

Tony didn't show any remorse toward the office closing. He just figured he now had to do what he had to do to get back on top. His mind stayed glued to what he had to do on the streets. Our relationship was still very distant after the night of that mission. Mainly because I couldn't look at him the same after knocking me out the way that he did. We hadn't even fucked in a while but I didn't even care.

Besides worrying about the company, I had Sharod's anniversary party coming up that I had to set up and I had a lot to do.

Two weeks had gone by and we closed down our mortgage company the Friday of week one. It was very sad and a lot of the employees were taken by surprise. I felt so bad, Susan actually cried but I told her that we would always stay in touch. She was a cool white chick and I had taken a liking to her over the years. But I knew I probably wouldn't be in touch with her unless I needed something. Shit, her pops was a cop I couldn't fuck with her like that knowing that Tony was hot.

The Saturday of Sharod's anniversary snuck up on us quite fast. The week before I had called around for different venues before locating the perfect spot to hold the celebration. I secured a large hall in Jamaica Plain which was perfect because most of Sharod's friends were still underage so it was no use in renting out a club.

A Hood Chick's Story Part II

Renee helped me set everything up for the party. We always did it up real big in Sharod's remembrance so that we could continue to keep his name alive in the hood. I got a big poster size picture of Sharod and had it hung high next to the words: "Rest in Peace, We miss you". I paid a few grand for a local Boston DJ Dru Nyce to host the party and I ordered catering from Bob the Chef's soul food.

The hall held about two hundred people but I was only expecting about fifty to seventy five. I wasn't too keen on having friends *of* friends there. It was strictly people who knew my little brother, my few friends and of course Trè's boys always came through to show their support. It was all love at the remembrance parties and I respected everyone who came through to show their love for my baby brother.

It was about noon when Renee and I put the finishing touches on the hall. We put all the table cloths on the tables, angled the chairs to the appropriate tables as well as along the walls. We spread silver confetti on the floor and let a few white helium filled balloons fly to the ceiling. I stood back and looked around at our hard work and after seeing that everything was to my satisfaction, Renee and I left. I dropped her off at home so that she could get herself together and do what she had to do before the party and I headed home.

I had a ritual that I had done every year since Sharod's passing. I would pour myself a glass of White

LaShonda DeVaughn

Zinfandel wine, sit inside of my living room in peace and quiet, turn off my cell phone and house phone ringer, pull out the photo album that I created with pictures of Sharod from when he was a baby up until the time he died and reminisce.

Tucked inside the album was the braid that I cut off his hair when he died and I would rub it with my thumb as I turned the pages of the album. This was my moment of mourning, my moment of remembrance, my time to cry. I would cry so hard that my ribs felt like they were caving into my stomach. I would occasionally laugh at some of his baby pictures remembering the good times that him, Trè, my mom and I shared when we were younger. It hurt that I couldn't have those years back. If I could give my right arm and leg to have them back I would cut them off myself.

After soaking dozens of tissues with tears, I completed my ritual. I headed to Shirley Max. The prison where Trè was serving his time and I would grieve with him. I mean, I knew that Trè was in jail and couldn't let other inmates see him shedding tears but we would talk through the whole visit about how we thought Sharod would be if he were still with us.

"Remember how he would always smile when he walked in the room? He always gave that sly smile and I wondered what he was up to," I said to Trè after we

A Hood Chick's Story Part II

exchanged hugs and small talk and then getting deep into our Sharod conversation.

Trè took a few seconds to answer because I could see his eyes drown into the wall visualizing Sharod. Trè was so tough and hardcore, but this broke him; losing Sharod fucked him up.

I stared at Trè's face waiting for his response. His face was all broken out in small bumps from being in the dirty prison system. He had dry blotches on his cheeks and his hair was dry and you could see the dandruff on the top of his old cornrows. His hair had grown about 2-3 inches and he'd gotten bigger, probably from lifting weights to pass the time.

After taking a long sigh, Trè finally replied.

"Sis, this shit is hard man. I miss Sharod like crazy and it ain't helping being in here. I be wanting to fuck niggas up for no reason. I'm hoping and praying to beat this appeal."

"Appeal?" I asked surprised. I normally knew everything about Trè's court business, I paid for his lawyer and everything. No one told me about an appeal.

Trè smiled. "I wanted to surprise you sis, my request for an appeal went through. There are holes in the evidence. When we got caught that night Big Renz told the jakes that he had did everything. That nigga was so down for the block, plus he knew how much losing Sharod meant to me. When

159

5-O surrounded us, he was in the car saying 'Trè I'll take the fall for this'. I mean I thought the nigga was talking out his ass but I also knew that he felt bad for a nigga. This is our little bro, niggas knew how hard that shit hit home feel me? But wanting to take the fall for all the hammers we had in the car was bananas. But he kept talking about how much work I put in for niggas so I respected his decision. But even with him taking the fall for the hammers, they still pinned this shit on me. Especially when they found out that the murders were linked for revenge."

Trè looked around to see if any of the Correction Officers were walking up before he continued.

"Come here sis." Trè signaled for me to sit up closer to him and I moved up toward him. "We tossed the burners we used on them niggas in the sewer before we got caught up. They didn't even catch us with the burners that killed them dudes. We just had so many guns in the car that night that they had to get us with something, plus they tried to say that I was a fuckin' career criminal, that's why they tried to add so many years to my shit. But the fact that they didn't catch us with the guns that killed them cowards left my case open for flaws. So pray for me sis, I'm 'bout to be off this soon."

I smiled big. I was so happy to hear that there was a chance for my big bro to come home.

A Hood Chick's Story Part II

"Wow, this brought some joy to my day bro, that's what's up."

Trè laughed. "So I'll be out to put my little sister in a head lock again," he said referring to how we used to fight in our younger days.

"Yeah whatever Trè, you're so silly. But on a serious note, if you get to come home, it would really do me some justice. I miss our family. I don't even know where Ma is, what kind of shit is that? Is she still rejecting your letters?"

Trè pursed up his lips.

"I don't send letters out anymore because they don't get forwarded to her new address; she put a stop to that. To be real with you T, at this point in my life, especially with me having a lot of time in here to think, I just put it like this, I don't have a mother or a father. We are on our own T and we're all we got, me you *and* Sharod, because his spirit lives in us."

Trè was dead serious; he had given up on our mom. And all of his so-called friends on the outside never visited him. No one sent him money unless I bumped into one of them on the streets then they would feel obligated to swing me whatever they had in their pockets to give to him. Other than that, they weren't thinking about him. That's how it was in the hood. When the top dog is on the outs, everyone respected him and professed how down they were for their

161

block. Once that top dog got locked up, you'd see just how many of them so-called friends would visit, put money on their phones or swing them canteen money. You would be lucky to get just one faithful visitor. Me on the other hand, loyalty was in my veins, I could never keep someone that I loved hanging.

The last thing that Trè said to me before leaving was that I needed to go get myself a gun license so that I would have protection in my house in case anything had ever happened. I told him how Tony had been asking me to do the same for months and that it was already taken care of. After that, I left.

I felt bad cutting the visit with Trè a little short but I had to go home and spend a little time with Shayonna before I packed her things to send her to Tony's aunt's house for the night. I also had to get myself together so that Tony and I would arrive at the hall on time.

A Hood Chick's Story Part II

The party was on and popping and everyone was having a good time enjoying the food and music.

Flirt with the hoodrats and then pop models! Everyone was amped to the tunes of Lil Wayne and Bird Man's song but no one danced but the females. Most of the niggas didn't dance in Boston anyway, they only played the walls. The most you'd see them doing is two stepping.

All of Sharod's friends showed up, well the one's that weren't locked up for minor hood shit, selling drugs, stolen cars or getting caught with a gun, the usual. Sharod's three closest friends who I remembered hanging with Sharod at my house back in the day always showed up. Every year they had a shirt with a different picture of Sharod on it and when the hall coordinators flicked off the lights, they all put up their lighters yelling out their blocks and shouting Sharod's name. I was proud that I was able to keep the parties live as if Sharod was right there partying with us, no one would ever forget my little soldier for sure.

I noticed that out of all of Sharod's friends, his three close friends, Mumbles, Kal and Turk had small writing in quotations on the back of their shirts. I pulled them aside to ask them what it stood for because I had never asked them before but I did remember seeing it on their shirts at the last anniversary.

Mumbles was a gunner, he was crazy as shit, his reputation on the streets was that he would bust his gun quick so if you don't pull yours out first, you already lost. He was as small as me but that didn't stop him from setting it with some of the biggest niggas.

Kal was laid back and very much into chicks. He was young, dumb and full of cum. He was only nineteen and had two kids by two different chicks and one on the way from a third. He thought that shit was cute too. But he was also known for robbing niggas. That little nigga stayed sticking niggas up.

Turk was always getting locked up. He spent much of his young life in the juvenile correctional system. Matter fact he got locked up a little after Sharod had died and he was in jail all fucked up over it.

"T, you just now seeing that writing on our shirts? We put that on the back of our Sharod shirts every year!" Mumbles shouted trying to yell over the music.

Mumbles was the closest of the three to Sharod. The three of them helped jump the boy that ended up taking Sharod's life. It was their very own friend who killed my brother. He tried to steal out of my mom's purse and they

164

whooped his ass. He couldn't take an old fashioned ass whopping and later ended up taking the life of my little brother and now my older brother Trè and his boys took his. This hood beef shit goes on and on, especially when someone gets killed. Unfortunately my family was a victim of the street statistics and the shit still weighs heavily within me.

"Let me talk to you over there for a second cause this shit's kinda deep?" Mumbles said pointing to a quieter spot near the restrooms; we left Kal and Turk by the wall and walked off.

The words on the back of their shirts read: *"Don't Cry, Just Ride!"* And I was dying to know what it symbolized.

"So what's up with that, why do y'all always put that on the back of your tee's?" I asked.

Mumbles leaned over and whispered in my ear. "When me, Sharod, Kal and Turk started getting into this street shit, we used to have long talks about dying; especially after we started putting in work. We always asked each other what we would do if one of us died. And you know how smooth Sharod was, he was straight to the point. He said to us: 'Dog if I die, don't cry, just ride'. And T, I will always remember that. So niggas are still riding for Sharod getting at that nigga's whole crew and whoever else is trying to retaliate for the nigga who took Rod." Mumbles lifted up his shirt to reveal the gun he had tucked in his jeans. But I was still stuck on what my little brother told them.

"Damn, that's deep Mumbles, y'all never told me that." I paused for a second drowning out the music in the club picturing Sharod saying the words *Don't Cry Just Ride* and it stuck in my head. When I regained my focus I had to set Mumbles straight, I cared about him and I didn't want anyone else getting into no more shit to make anyone else lose their life.

"Mumbles, make sure you, Kal and Turk stay safe man. This street shit ain't worth it. It keeps going back and forth and the shit makes no sense. Y'all just focus on getting money that's what Sharod would have wanted a'ight?"

Mumbles was still fired up thinking about Sharod, I'm sure my words didn't sink in because the little nigga was crazy but I had hoped that he heard me.

"A'ight T." he said.

These little nigga's had their own agenda but I always gave my advice even if they didn't take heed. They were my little homey's and I wanted them safe. I didn't care if they felt like I lost my hood appeal, I just finally had a grasp on life and the streets weren't going to take control any longer, I was taking control and the streets wouldn't win again, I hoped.

"There you are T, I been looking for you," Renee said. Mumbles mingled back over to his friends and I walked

166

off with Renee. She took my hand and began leading me to a back room in the hall.

"Girl why are we going back here, what's back here?"

I looked around at the grit and grime on the walls; it was so nasty back there it seemed as if we walked into another building. I didn't know what the fuck Renee was up to.

We finally reached a white door that Renee had to bump her ass on to open. As soon as she opened it, I walked in behind her.

"Surprise," Renee said in a shaky voice. There on the corroded old couches sat my old friends Ke-Ke and Karen. They both stood to acknowledge me and then greeted me at the same time.

"Hey T," they said in unison.

I haven't seen Ke-Ke and Karen in years. I damn sure never thought that I would see the both of them in the same room together. They wanted to take each other's heads off over dirty dick Shawn. He had infected them both with crabs and the last I heard about the Karen and Ke-Ke situation was that they bumped into each other at the Copley mall and was about to get it on until security separated them both. Seeing them together only made me assume that they squashed it.

Ke-Ke's appearance was different, I mean, no one could wear stress well, but with her, stress showed in her face profusely. Her pretty face was now riddled with dents and enlarged bags under her eyes. When I looked at her stomach, I noticed that her gut was sitting out almost as far out as her donkey ass so I assumed that she must have a seed or two. Plus her lips were black as if she smoked as much as Tony. Overall, she looked bad.

Karen looked exactly the same. She tried to smile through her screw face when she greeted me but I could tell that she was the same bitch. I felt kind of awkward seeing my old friends. We were so close when we were young, bitches couldn't tell us nothing. Funny how friendships could end over men, petty arguments or unnecessary drama. If you really think about it, nothing is worth losing good friends or real friends for that matter. I kept my distance through the years because I needed to get my mind right after losing Sharod. Renee was basically my only friend during the time that I challenged the hardest years of my life without my family.

Before I said anything to Karen and Ke-Ke, I glanced over at Renee. She had a sly look on her face.

"Don't kill me T, but I did call them. They felt bad after not being there for you over the years after losing Sharod. So we thought this was the perfect place for us to squash everything."

A Hood Chick's Story Part II

I watched as everyone waited for my reaction, Ke-Ke and Karen didn't know what to expect and finally I cracked a smile. They all reacted the same and then rushed over to hug me at the same time.

We all laughed, cried and were so involved in missing each other that the moment became overly emotional. It all felt right though, we picked right up where we left off.

When we returned from the back room and re-entered the hall area, I saw Tony looking at us curiously. I could tell he was wondering where the fuck Ke-Ke and Karen came out the cut from. He often reminded me over the years how happy he was that I cut off my "hoodrat" friends.

I made my way over to him and before he could ask me anything I told him that I would explain later. Ke-Ke and Karen both waved at Tony but he just looked at them like they had four heads. He couldn't stand them.

The DJ started playing the Gucci Mane track "She's A Very Freaky Girl" and Tony bobbed his head putting his hands up.

"This is my shit," he said.

Ke-Ke, Karen and Renee roamed off to dance with some of Trè's friends and I grooved with Tony. He loved Gucci Mane, that's mostly what he played in his car. Gucci Mane and UGK. And when Pimp C died, it was like Tony lost a family member, he was pissed. But he loved any rapper that rapped about hustling because that's all he's ever known.

The night ended up being a success. There was no violence just a peaceful celebration.

Tony was to the meat! He was staggering around from having too many shots of Patròn so he had his friend Cat drive his Beamer. I was straight enough to drive my whip plus I had no choice. Ke-Ke and Karen got dropped off by someone and had no way of getting back home. I wondered how they would have gotten home if I hadn't accepted their little peace treaty but it was just like them to gamble on some shit like that. Not only that but when we got in the car, Ke-Ke told me she lived further away from the hood then I did. She moved to Fall River with her new boyfriend so I would have to go out of my way to drop her ass off. It was cool though, we all needed this time in the car to catch up on things.

A Hood Chick's Story Part II

Chapter Twelve – Can't Be Trusted

I pulled out of my parking spot and headed toward Washington Street to drop Karen off first.

"Now y'all know I'm gonna put y'all on the spot right?" I looked in my rearview mirror at Ke-Ke and Karen while driving. Renee secured her position in the passenger seat and she was a little more than tipsy.

"So, when did y'all squash the beef?" I finally asked.

They both started speaking at the same time and then Karen sat back and let Ke-Ke say her part first.

"Well first of all, you might as well say we squashed it tonight. Renee hit me up telling me where you were throwing Sharod's bash at and she told me that she was also calling Karen and I was like fuck it, it's cool, that bullshit we went through is old."

Karen cut her off, "Same thing I said, when Renee called me and said that we would all be there together, I told her that it was cool and I wouldn't disrespect Sharod's party

171

anyway. Plus I felt bad for not being there for you through the years, I let you have your space but it's time I came to support my girl."

"Are you serious, y'all hadn't spoken before tonight?" I asked.

I was shocked to know that this was the first time they'd seen each other. We were all so comfortable with each other, it was as if we'd never lost touch. You would have never had guessed that they hadn't squashed their beef before then. But it goes to show that some friends can keep an unbreakable bond even if there were past problems.

"Plus we were young back then. I ain't gonna front though, I caught feelings for Shawn that's why it fucked me up." Ke-Ke spoke whole heartedly.

As she spoke, she starting to think deeper into the situation and was now looking at Karen while venting. "Yeah I know I always told y'all that I had no feelings for none of the dudes I was messing with at the time, but Karen, you and everyone else knew how I felt about Shawn and that shit hurt when you backstabbed me, straight up."

Karen took in each word and then surprised us all. "You got that, I was in the wrong for what I did and I apologize."

"Hold the fuck up!" I said pretending to have a heart attack. "Did I just hear the Queen bitch apologize to someone? Renee you hear this?" I asked sarcastically.

A Hood Chick's Story Part II

Renee peeked back at Karen from the passenger seat and we all started laughing. Ke-Ke and Karen then hugged in the backseat and it felt good to see it.

Although their situation was grimy, I was glad that they came to terms of squashing it, even more, I was the mediator and didn't even know it so we truly needed each other, no matter how old we got. Shawn wasn't shit anyway; he was not worth their friendship.

When they finished hugging, they wiped a few tears and then began joking about the situation.

"Shit, he gave us crabs anyway, it wasn't even worth it," Karen said.

"Giiirl, I was so mad at him for that, I had them little muthafuckas crawling around my toilet seat and I didn't know what the fuck was going on." Ke-Ke's crazy ass blurted out demonstrating with her fingers.

"Ughhhhh!!" Renee and I shouted like we felt the crabs crawling on our skin.

"We don't wanna hear about y'all's STD situations, but I'll tell you this much, Shawn is still the same," I said.

"Oh I'm sure he is." Ke-Ke agreed. "That's why I stay sucka free, no more niggas like Shawn would get near me. But this new dude I'm with, his name is Jerry."

"Wait a minute, you settled down my nigga?" Renee's drunk ass asked curiously.

"I didn't say all that Renee." Ke-Ke said chuckling, "But Jerry is nice, he treats me right and I really can't complain about him except for he don't got money like that. When I first got with him, he was doing his thing out here; he made money for real, for real. He caught a case and ever since he's been on probation he had to get a job and it just ain't working for me man. I can't be with no broke dude. He don't have no skills so the punk ass job that he has ain't doing shit. I can do bad by myself."

"So why you with him if you ain't happy? You got any kids by him?" I asked. Judging from her gut, I figured she had at least one or two seeds.

"Hell no I don't have no kids by him? But where else am I going to go? I moved in with him in Fall River and I guess you can say I'm comfortable but I'm not happy though."

"Same with me," Karen exclaimed. "I don't have a man right now because it's hard. Every dude I meet got some shit with him, either he has kids and baby mama drama, no job, he's a cornball or he's too cocky or too broke. I'm picky when it comes to niggas. Why can't I meet a thugged out doctor or lawyer? All the educated dudes are usually cornballs and I couldn't see myself with no house nigga. I need a dude to tell me to shut the fuck up sometimes, I can't have no dude asking if he can watch Lifetime with me. I want a nigga that rocks a business suit

A Hood Chick's Story Part II

during the day and then changes into his Timbs y'all feel me?"

"Hell Yeah." Ke-Ke screamed out first.

We all agreed with Karen on that last note. I also started thinking about Tony because Karen's ideal man was who I used to have at home. I loved the fact that Tony had a real job and left the street life alone when he had opened up the Mortgage Company, I used to feel so lucky. It was very rare finding a dude with a real job, a real job that made money for that matter from the hood. It was farfetched and security was a factor that every chick from the hood tried to secure. And if we didn't find it, most chicks just settled and would end up with a low life dead beat or just plain unhappy like Ke-Ke, I loved her to death but she was still the same, just older. In other words Ke-Ke was a grown up hoodrat. She told us how she had a few abortions by Jerry and her ass had the nerve to wait until she was four months pregnant to do it. So I guess that explained her gut, after all them abortions, the bulge just never left.

I could still see and hear the bitchiness in Karen but something in her had changed. For some reason I got the impression that she wanted to better herself by the vibe she was giving off and I was usually pretty good at reading people.

LaShonda DeVaughn

"What about you T, I see you doing big things, this fly ass car and that big ass rock on your finger, you always had your head on right though. But when's the wedding?"

"Yeah!" Karen shouted waiting for the answer along with Ke-Ke.

I gave them chick's a look in the rear view mirror. "When he learns how to keep his dick in his pants, then maybe, MAYBE I'll think about marrying his ass."

I stopped myself in my own tracks. I had got ahead of myself and suddenly I regretted confessing my business to my girls. We had a bit more catching up to do for me to be spilling out my personal life like that. I never knew who really had good intentions in mind for me. Either way, I had to game face my old friends first.

"What! Tony's stepping out on you T? Oh hell no, he done lost his mind, he got a good chick! Let me find out I have to bring it to Tony." Ke-Ke shouted.

"Shit, that's why I won't be faithful to no nigga. For what? So you can put your heart and soul into one man and let him have you thinking you're the Queen of the world until you find out that your man has about three or four other hoes thinking that they are the Queen of the world too. Fuck that, it's money over niggas for me." Ke-Ke said.

"That's some spicy shit you just kicked there my nigga," Karen said dapping Ke-Ke up agreeing with her to the fullest. Renee's drunk ass looked back agreeing as well.

176

A Hood Chick's Story Part II

"Y'all hoes are crazy," I said.

"Please T, I know all kinds of niggas be out here trying to holla at you, he better wise up. And I know how you are too, you're probably out here shutting them all down and being faithful," Ke-Ke said.

I laughed. "Girl you got me down packed. But what I look like hollering at other dudes if we are still together? I don't get why some girls think that way. It's like you get mad at the nigga for dogging you and sleeping with Keisha, Monique and Suzy, but then you're out there sleeping with Joe, Bob and Rick too; so why get mad at him? It's contradicting. I don't even have it in me to step out of the relationship and sell my soul because of his mistakes. He cheated, not me, so why should I belittle myself and cheat on him? I would just leave him if I wanted someone else.

"That's what niggas need to do instead of cheating on chicks, just don't get in a relationship. Let her know like yo, I don't want to be in a relationship and yes I'm doing other broads on the side so that it would be up to that chick if she wants to settle for a dude that's out here dick hopping or not. I would respect an honest dude rather than a dude that keeps cheating and then lying about it. If I would have known from the beginning that I would go through all of this bullshit I'm going through, I would have been a single chick." I ended.

177

"Come on now though T, what dude you know that will say that?" Karen asked and everyone else agreed with her.

"Oh trust me y'all, some dudes are honest from jump and tells the chick that they rather be friends and don't want to settle down, but like I said, I don't condone it, but at least they let the chick know that it's her choice to be stupid enough to keep fucking him without the title or leaving him be."

I kinda felt that I may have been offending all three of my homegirls in the car but I had to keep it real. I wasn't for all that sneaking around bullshit; it was nothing cute about it to me. I also wasn't passing judgment on any of them, they were their own woman and could do as they pleased; I just always tried to set high standards for myself. Plus I wanted stability in my life. My past was too staggered to continue on this path. I needed something rock solid, a foundation that would keep me sane and keep me focused or else I would be a lost cause. Plus I had a daughter and it would be improper to let her see me with daddy and then the next man and the next man, HELL no!

I kept driving toward Karen's spot. She'd moved in with her Aunt in the South End in the Cathedral projects. She said her mom felt like she was too old to be home and that she was done raising children and told Karen that she had to go so that she could have her own life with her

A Hood Chick's Story Part II

boyfriend. Her mom always has been grimy. She and Karen used to bump heads so much when we were younger. Her mom was the true bitch and Karen inherited her traits. And I'm not saying that to be disrespectful, her mom was off the hook, she would call Karen bitches and sluts for no reason; it was crazy. But I was happy that she didn't live at the old spot anyway because we were neighbors in the same building where I lived with my mom and brothers. I swear I tried to avoid that building and it's memories as much as possible. But I did wanna know what was happening in the streets.

"So what's been poppin' in the hood lately?" I asked feeling out of touch. I knew that Ke-Ke and Karen kept their ears to the street, it was in their nature, plus they were nosy.

"Oh I got a lot to update y'all on." Ke-Ke said smirking through her screw face like she was about to tell us some good gossip.

"Word, put us on," I said.

"Okay first, y'all remember that dude Jason? You know that nigga you used to do scams and shit with T, the dude that used to be in love with you, but you always dissed him?"

"Yeah I remember him," I said.

"Well I seen that nigga recently and he was walking with a strut meaner than mine. He was in Macy's downtown

179

shopping and walking around all dramatically like he was trying to rip the run way."

We all started cracking the fuck up.

"Yeah right Ke-Ke." I said in disbelief.

"Girl if I'm lying I'm flying, y'all know I mean mugged him and didn't want his fruity ass to come nowhere near me, he looked a hot a mess. He even had on lipstick and eyeliner. You know he don't show his face in the hood no more cause niggas would stomp the shit outta him."

It was so weird to hear that a dude from the hood had switched and went the other way. I didn't know too many gay dudes, especially from the hood, it was rare and that shit shocked all of us. Also to hear that it was Jason was even more shocking. He tried to take advantage of me when I was younger and I never told anyone. Guess his way of staying in the closet back then was trying to rape chicks, but damn he's gay now, it's still unbelievable.

"Yooooo, speaking of that, y'all ain't' gonna believe what I heard," Karen said after our laughter calmed down.

"What!" We all asked as a trio rushing Karen along.

"Guess who I heard is a straight dike now?"

"Who!" Renee's drunk ass shouted.

"A'ight y'all ready for this?"

"Yeah we ready bitch, who?" Renee asked again.

"Shavon!" Karen jumped out of her seat when she let the name out and we all screamed.

A Hood Chick's Story Part II

I just couldn't believe it. Shavon was a part of our crew growing up; she was one of the top chicks knocking bitches out whenever we had problems. Then she just disappeared when she got a little bit of change in her pockets and acted like we never had her back out here. She left us all hanging and moved away and never contacted us again.

"Yup, I heard that she's gay." Karen smirked.

"Yo that's crazy, I can't even picture that, I mean she always carried herself like a dude because she was always fighting but she was always into big funny looking niggas, I wonder what changed her." I pictured Shavon in my head and memories appeared when we were all tight back in the day, she was my homey and I actually started to miss her while thinking about her.

"Damn let me find out that Shavon is a carpet muncher," I said.

Everyone started laughing and holding their bellies.

I pulled up to the curb on the side of the Cathedral projects to let Karen out and before she got out, she looked back puzzled.

"Yo, what is a carpet muncher anyway?"

Everyone laughed at Karen being naïve but she had a straight face and really wanted the answer.

"A'ight, put it like this," I started. "Get in the shower, look down and then let Ke-Ke come in there and munch on your carpet."

181

We all started rolling and Karen got out the car calling me crazy, but she now knew what the definition meant.

"A'ight T, I'll call you, I got your number from Renee, y'all be safe."

"A'ight, bye Karen." We all blurted out before pulling off.

My next stop was Renee's spot. We continued to catch up with each other in the car.

"So T, how long was Tony locked up and when did he get out?" Ke-Ke asked.

"Tony was locked up for three years and he's been out for two."

"So you kept your shit tight for three years?" she asked.

"You know I did." I said.

"You're my fuckin' hero," Ke-Ke said tapping my shoulder.

Renee's drunk ass sat up.

"Yo Ke-Ke, when Tony was locked up, I used to have mad niggas coming to the spot, sometimes the niggas would be fly and I be like T, come out with us, get your feet wet a little bit and get yourself broke off. Her ass would give me that serious look she be giving us when she be blitzing on niggas and I just used to be like fuck it."

I cut her drunk ass the fuck off.

182

A Hood Chick's Story Part II

"Renee, first of all you never brought no fly niggas to the crib when I lived with you. They were all crusty dust ball niggas. Plus I was too focused to be having some niggas on my mind. I was stressed, depressed and broke. My focus was on my daughter Shayonna and on some real shit, I don't think that I would have survived losing Sharod if it wasn't for my daughter."

"Aw T I know that was rough for you. And I want to meet your daughter, I know she's beautiful," Ke-Ke said.

"My daughter's the shit," I boasted.

We all chuckled and Renee agreed. "She is a cutie Ke-Ke."

"Oh I'm sure she is," Ke-Ke said before adding, "She's the newest DPG member, a tiny Dime Piece Gangstress."

"She got the sassiness for it," Renee said.

"Whatever y'all my baby is far from a little gangstress."

We had fun growing up claiming our little crew. DPG would never be forgotten around my old way. Everyone remembered us for smashing chicks that crossed us. I even heard there were younger girls from around my old way claiming DPG now. I used to think it was cute, but if they are anything like we were when we were growing up, God help those little girls because they are nothing trouble.

LaShonda DeVaughn

Ke-Ke sat back and the car was quiet for a little while until her horny ass just couldn't help but to ask some more sexual shit.

"I just still can't believe you kept your legs closed for three years. What the hell were you doing to get off? You must have been wearing your little silver bullet out."

"What the fuck is a silver bullet?" I asked. I had never used any sex toys before so I had no clue.

"I know your just playing right?" Ke-Ke asked sitting up.

"That bullet is the shit!" Renee blurted out putting her hands up like she was preaching to the choir.

"Girl, go to the sweet and nasty store and buy you a bullet, you will probably never need Tony again. Shit, since you don't like cheating you should buy you a bullet so you can feel like your cheating on his ass when he acts up."

"I'm bout to go home and use my bullet now, my shit vibrates maximum speed," Renee said closing her eyes as drunk as she wanted to be.

"Y'all are so nasty. I'm good, I won't be needing no silver bullets any time soon."

"Well I'm just putting you on girl," Ke-Ke said.

We were finally at Renee's crib and she staggered her drunk ass to the front door.

"You gon' be a'ight Renee, you want me to walk you to your apartment?"

A Hood Chick's Story Part II

"I'm good T, I'll talk to you tomorrow."

"A'ight Renee good night."

After dropping off Renee, Ke-Ke jumped in the front seat.

"I couldn't wait till you dropped her off." She said.

"Why?" I asked suspiciously while pulling away.

"Well, what do you think about her new job?" she asked with her lips twisted to the side.

"New job? Renee's lazy ass didn't tell me about no new job? A new job doing what?"

"Now T, I haven't been in touch with y'all in years, so I hope I don't know what she does and you don't?" Ke-Ke said.

"Well put me on bitch, I don't know what you're talking about."

"Okay, well you know that dude Tank from Renee's projects right?"

I smirked. "Yeah I know his lame ass."

"You know what he does right?" Ke-Ke asked as if I should have known.

"No, but I know his whack ass be putting his hands on chicks."

"You know why right?"Ke-Ke said.

"Yeah because he's a fuckin' coward."

"No bitch, he's a pimp."

"Whaaat?" I almost crashed my damn car.

185

LaShonda DeVaughn

"A pimp?"

"Yeah girl, he be pimping Renee. He got a few chicks from Fall River working for him. I went to school with one of the chicks, she lives in my apartment complex. Tank be coming out there paying for their spot and making sure their stank asses break him off his paper and if they come up short, he be fuckin' them up. And when I say fuckin' them up, them bitches be having big ass Tina Turner bruises on them."

"Oh hell nah," I hollered.

"Yeah girl I guess Renee turned being a chickenhead into a full time job, haaa."

"Nah Ke, that's not funny."

"You right it ain't but when ole' girl told me about Renee, I started tripping! I was hoping that Renee had changed but she went ass backwards."

Ke-Ke didn't know it but she had just put me on to some valuable shit that would probably end me and Renee's friendship. I'm sure Renee didn't tell me about her new occupation because she felt ashamed of it. But damn, that right there should tell you something; if you're ashamed of it, then you shouldn't be doing it. But the bigger picture was, I not only jeopardized myself but also niggas from Trè's block thinking that I was helping a friend and all that I was doing was digging myself deeper into some street shit that I should've just minded my business about. So there I sat,

186

backstabbed once again. She really let me take it as far as getting niggas after Tank knowing the whole time that she would go back to Tank since she worked for him. She lied about why he hit her, she knew she must've came up short on his money and that's why he was so-called setting her straight by whooping her ass.

"Niggas out here be killing me like they Iceberg Slim, they be having girlfriends still trying to pimp some loose booty bitches on the side. You can't live the pimp life and the square life, pick one nigga!" I said as if I was talking to Tank.

"Yup T, I agree. Do he still go with that pretty chick Bianca?"

"Yup he sure do," I replied.

"Shit, I wonder if she knows that he be out here pimping. And if she do know, I know he probably lied to her and told her he ain't fuckin' his hoes but he is digging in all their asses because the girls in my apartment complex be telling me and I know for a fact Renee's nasty ass be letting him up in that."

"Man Ke, I ain't got time for this, I can't believe Renee man, I'm pissed off right now."

"Don't be pissed off, she'll learn, I don't know what it's gonna take but she will definitely learn. Fuckin' mad different niggas and giving all of her money to Tank is just stupid to me. I don't know how chicks could do it. If I fuck for money, he would have to give me that gwap in my hands and I would be damned if I would give my doe up to some so-called pimp dude, hell no, not Ke-Ke baby."

I was so fired up at the fact that Renee had lied to me to the point where I was now speeding up the highway and reached Ke-Ke's crib in no time.

Her house was right off the exit, I pulled up and put the car in park. I noticed Ke-Ke was grinning looking at her front door. "Ugh, I hate going in this house with this broke dude, a nigga with no money is such a turn off." She said while rolling her eyes.

She lifted up her purse. "Look at this shit T. This is a bootleg Gucci bag. Since when have you known me to rock fake shit like this?"

"Ke-Ke you're a mess, you're just used to having nice shit. He's probably a good dude, you better stop treating him bad before you lose him and end up with a cheater or someone who treats you like shit."

"You might be right but broke just ain't cute," she said screwing up her face to the max.

"Bitch get out my car with your crazy ass," I said chuckling.

Ke-Ke smiled and then bent to hug me. "Girl I missed you so much it's not even funny Tiara. I'm sorry about everything too, you were truly the only real friend that I had and I never really realized that till you were gone."

A Hood Chick's Story Part II

"I missed you too girl. We could have all squashed this a long time ago but I just needed to get my mind right. I was so focused when I lived with Renee, nothing else mattered. And when Tony got out, I tried to start my life out fresh and I was actually happy again, but now it seems like I'm being pulled backwards in some ways. But we'll talk later girl, get in the house to your man, I'll holla at you."

"A'ight T, I love you."

"Love you to."

I drove home steaming thinking about Renee. Tank just got shot and now the war is going to continue to go back and forth between him and Trè's block and I was very much a part of it. And just like that I put myself back into some hood shit over a friend.

I was heated with myself for making a stupid decision trying to have someone hurt this dude for my homegirl and she knew damn well why he hit her. I was truly moving backwards instead of forward and I had to get it together quick. First things first, I had to check Renee's ass.

"Hello?"

"Yo Renee it's me, Tiara. I have to talk to you."

"A'ight T hold on for a second, I'm in here throwing up, I drank too much tonight and didn't eat shit all day."

She put me on hold and I heard her gagging in the background but I didn't care, she was gonna feel me tonight!

"A'ight T what's up?"

189

"What's up is you! Why didn't you tell me what you *really* be fuckin' with Tank for?" I got straight to the point.

She fell silent. Check mate!

"Hello? Nigga you heard me," I griped.

She sighed. "T, why you coming at me like that let me explain?"

"I'm listening, explain this shit to me."

"Okay man damn, how did you find out?"

"Fuck that, what's your explanation Renee?"

"Well T, first off I'm grown, I really don't have to explain shit to you but you're my girl so I'm gonna tell you since you're putting it on the table. Yeah I been dealing with Tank, I'm getting money with him."

"Getting money with him how Renee?"

"Damn, why do I have to say all that if you already know?"

"Because it's fucked up that's why. How you gonna have me put Ken-Ken into this when you knew all along why Tank hit you? That's fucked up Renee. Now you got me in some shit and if my name comes up in this, it could really get ugly out here, niggas could try to off me when all I was trying to do was help you out because you're my girl."

"T, you got yourself in this shit don't blame me."

"Oh it's like that? I got myself in this shit? That's real fucked up Renee, you knew the deal before we went to

A Hood Chick's Story Part II

Trè's block, you could have told me not to tell them to do shit to Tank."

"Why you think I asked you to give me Ken-Ken's number afterward, you really thought I wanted to kick it with him on some being my man shit? I wanted to tell him not to touch Tank."

"So why didn't you just tell *me* that?"

"Because I didn't want you to know what I was doing."

"All these years Renee, you held me down when I had no one and it takes this one thing to fuck us up. I can't fuck with you no more man, shit like this just pulls me backwards. I love you to death but this is some shit that I don't think I can forgive."

"Well I ain't gonna hold your hand, you're a grown woman, you want to end our friendship over this then fuck it."

"You're right Renee, fuck it."

I clicked her off and threw my cell into my passenger seat. And just like that, I ended our friendship immediately. As they say, with friends like her, who needed enemies.

LaShonda DeVaughn

Chapter Thirteen – The Mistake

Tony began to question my whereabouts because I spent the majority of my days handling my property. My time was solely spread between Shayonna and my obligations as a new property owner. After Shayonna completed her homework each day, it was either Chuck E. Cheese or out to see a Disney movie and I enjoyed every second spent with my baby.

Business with my property consisted of making new leases for each floor, obtaining deleaded certificates and also ensuring that each apartment was in tip-top condition for showings. I was extremely proud of how things were coming along because I was just steps closer to generating income from the tenants and wouldn't have to depend on Tony for shit.

Tony offered to take Shayonna and I out to eat because he claimed that he'd been missing us because of his absence from the crib spent hustling. I rejected his offer and instead took Shayonna with me to the Lee School in

A Hood Chick's Story Part II

Dorchester with Karen to watch her little cousin perform at a talent show.

The Lee School was known for throwing hot talent shows and it was also a school and recreational center for youths. I loved attending their talent shows because they always had an array of creative, talented and diverse performers. There were often rappers, dancers and singers showcasing their talents and there were always large turnouts. I loved watching the dancers mainly because they always brought the most excitement to the talent shows and Karen's little cousin Nick could dance his ass off.

The DJ began playing a mix of Crank Dat, Souljah Boy and Walk It Out and the crowd went wild as Nick's dance group entered the stage with full energy.

"Yeah Nick!" Karen's loud mouth hollered out along with other rowdy audience members and onlookers.

The boys came out and started Crunk dancing against each other. They were doing dance moves pretending to hit each other, popping their bodies in wild motions. The shit was off the hook.

My brother Sharod would have been the same age as the boys dancing if he were still alive and it just killed me that he was no longer here. Karen's little cousin Nick was into sports and he also danced as a hobby. The extra activities helped keep him off the streets and he was known as a good dude. I sat wishing that I could have motivated my little brother to participate in some sort of extra activity so that he wouldn't have to had spend so much time in the streets mixing in with the wrong crowds.

Watching Nick's crew perform crushed my heart thinking about Sharod so much to the point that I wanted to leave. I was truly zoned out. That was until my baby girl stood up and started Crunking. It was too cute, Shayonna was moving her little body to the beats and we had our own little show going on in the audience. She was frowning up her lips like she was in a Ciara video giving her "dance face" swaying her hips, popping and dancing better than some of the kids in the show. I didn't even know my baby's little body could pop like that, dance school was paying off.

"Go Shayonna! Go Shayonna!" Karen and I chimed out dancing along with her.

We actually ended up having a ball at the talent show.

My daughter added so much joy to my life, it was little things like her dancing in the midst of me drowning in my grief that helped me out and she had no idea. She really made my day that day.

Tony called my cell on our way out and told me that he at least wanted to spend time with Shayonna since I gave him the cold shoulder earlier. So after we left the Lee School I dropped Shayonna off at home to spend some time with her father while I took Karen home.

A Hood Chick's Story Part II

As I mentioned before, I noticed something inside Karen that changed but I just couldn't put my finger on it until she decided to pour her heart out to me.

"You a'ight Karen?" She got quiet all of a sudden.

"Yeah I'm a'ight."

"You sure girl?"

"Yeah I'm good; I just hate living with my aunt. I'm too old to be living there with her. All of her kids already moved out and I'm sitting in there like an asshole eating her food and drinking her shit, you don't understand what that shit does to my pride."

"It's cool girl it's only temporary, you'll get on your feet soon," I said hitting the back roads to her crib.

"Shit that sounds good T. The only good thing about living with my aunt is that I'm out of my mother's house. She kicked me out because she wanted to be with her young ass boyfriend. She calls him her pretty young thang. But girl, that man has been molesting me for years." She looked down and shook her head before she went on. "It seemed like my mom always knew that he had a thang for me and that's why she always treated me like shit. I know you remember how she was when we were young T? She acted like she resented me for living, like she meant for my father to cum on her face instead of inside her to produce me."

"Don't say no crazy shit like that." I sympathized.

LaShonda DeVaughn

"I'm serious; T come on now my mother was a bitch. She hated me for a long time and that's why I'm the way that I am. I have this shell that people can't crack because I don't trust anyone. I never had many friends besides y'all because no one ever understood me. The way that I carry myself chases people away because I'm always so hard.

"But once I moved out, I realized that I didn't need to carry an attitude like I hated the world because it wasn't my fault that her boyfriend was touching on me when she wasn't looking, I couldn't control him, I could only control myself. That's why I'm trying to be a better person T, I used to blame myself for what happened to me but now I'm not blaming myself anymore and I'm taking it one day at a time."

"That's what's up Karen. I'm glad you have a positive attitude about the situation. And I'm so sorry to hear that he was doing that to you, I had no idea. I honestly believe that everything happens for a reason, you went through that pain and instead of wanting to continue to walk around like the world owes you something, you want to change and I applaud you for that. One thing that my mother used to always say to me is 'Tiara don't be like me, be better than me' so show and prove Karen. Be better than your mother not like her. And from this situation, you got strength out of it instead of weakness."

A Hood Chick's Story Part II

"I'm trying T, I really am." She said nodding.

"And that's all that you can do homey is try because trust when I say, everything is going to be alright you hear me?"

Karen shook her head and cried. It was the first time I'd seen her shed the amount of tears that she had. Her hard exterior was now softening and it was a good thing.

I always hated to see someone that I cared about in pain. Sometimes I felt as though I took on everyone else's problems ignoring my own. But I had to step in. I know that Karen, Ke-Ke and I had lost touch for years but I still loved them as if they'd never left and I had to be there for them.

The very next day I picked them both up and told them that I had a surprise for them.

"Where are we going T?" Ke-Ke asked for the fifth time.

"You'll see we're almost there." I was so excited to show them what I had for them that I was speeding down the highway and the side streets. I had learned so many backstreets from riding dirty in the streets with Tony that it was so usual for me to take backstreets instead of main roads.

At last, I pulled up and parked in front of my property.

"Who lives here?" Karen said gazing up the three story house.

"Just come on!" I said excitedly pulling out my keys to lead them up to the second floor.

"Surprise!"

The two of them walked in and looked around.

"What's the surprise?" Ke-Ke asked.

"I own this house, I'm giving ya'll both this apartment to share. It's a three bedroom, what y'all think?"

"Yeah right?" Karen let out first. Ke-Ke put her hand on her head looking at the new moldings and Newpro windows.

"What would I tell Jerry?" she blurted out. It took her one minute literally to dwell on Jerry and then she said, "You know what fuck him, I'm moving my shit in today!"

They both ran around flicking on the lights in the eat-in kitchen and large living room and then checked out the bathroom.

"T, we love you!!" They both ran up to me hugging me almost knocking me down. I was so happy that I was able to help them out. I was just hoping that my nice gesture wasn't a mistake.

Now I'd never met Ke-Ke's boyfriend Jerry, but whoever homeboy was, I felt sorry for him. Ke-Ke left him immediately and had all of her belongings settled into the new spot within a weeks time. She and Karen were so excited about their new living situation that they were like sisters again. They would call me from Wal-Mart to tell me about the different color towels and wall sconces they were buying to put up in the bathroom or the drapes that they wanted to put inside the living room. It was really good to hear the happiness coming from the both of them. I was glad that I was a part of making things in their lives easier. They had both been through a lot and deserved it. Renee on the other hand was cut, so I distanced myself from her and of course so did the girls.

I finally found some tenants for the first and third floor whom I felt were trustworthy. I performed credit and background checks to see if they had a stable work and credit history. I had to thoroughly check them both out in hopes that they were able to afford the place and have rent in my hand not a day shorter than the first of the month. I collected two thousand dollars from both floors and only five hundred dollars collectively from Ke-Ke and Karen monthly. I knew Ke-Ke and Karen couldn't afford the spot so two hundred and fifty a piece shouldn't be a problem. They both had no jobs and I had no idea where they were getting the money from and I was afraid to ask.

There was a young couple that occupied the first floor. They had a one year old daughter and a three year old boy. They both held great jobs and had solid landlord references as well as good standing in their occupations so I was delighted to welcome them in. The couple seemed really happy with each other too. They didn't seem like they were from around my old neighborhood, which meant they weren't hood at all. They probably grew up around the Quincy area but they seemed decent and to themselves. The young lady's boyfriend was actually a cutie, he was an Accountant so homegirl had her a good man. Of course I had to tell Ke-Ke and Karen to keep their eyes and hands off him. I didn't want any drama.

The third floor was occupied by an Asian couple. It was just a husband and wife but the wife was expecting their first child. They drove a CLK that was similar to the car that Tony bought me so I knew that I wouldn't have any problems with getting my rent from them.

Things went smooth for about two months. I collected the rent, paid the mortgage and kept the rest of the money to lace me and Shayonna. Tony would often look at me odd wondering where I got the money from to refurbish my entire wardrobe. But on the other hand most of it was going in the bank. Before my new tenants moved in, I collected, first and last months rent from them so that was eight grand that I immediately put in the bank.

It all changed the night I got a phone call at two in the morning. Of course Tony was just coming in the house from a night of hustling and he was settling into our bedroom.

I answered my phone and the heard the caller breathing heavily through the other end.

A Hood Chick's Story Part II

"Hi, is this Tiara?"

"Yes it is, who's calling?"

"This is your tenant on the first floor, can you come out here please?"

She was crying so I knew that it was important but like I said, it was two in the damn morning.

"Can it wait for tomorrow?" I asked.

I heard her sniffling. "No, you really need to come out here now."

I told her that I was on my way and hung up the phone pissed off about having to get up out of my sleep. But I was a landlord so this was my job.

Tony was taking off his shoes about to get comfortable but he overheard a little of my conversation.

"Who the fuck was that?" he asked.

"No one," I replied.

I hopped up and threw on some clothes.

"Where are you going Tiara?" he asked demanding an answer.

"Nowhere, I'm just going to check on Karen and Ke-Ke."

I fed him short answers in hopes that he would mind his business.

"Oh here we go! So those hoodrats are calling my girl at two in the morning to put you into some of their drama? Why are you still fucking with those mud-ducks anyway, I never liked either one of them."

I ignored Tony, I had to go and see what was going on. Plus I wanted to hurry up and get back home and get to bed. I was tired as fuck and Quincy was about twenty five minutes from my crib so I was pissed that I had to take that drive at that hour.

When I pulled up to the curb, I went from sleepy to pissed all in the blink of an eye. The ambulance, Quincy police and a shit load of neighbors were outside. I got out of the car and ran up to one of the officers.

"Excuse me what's going on?" I asked.

The officer looked at me and didn't answer. I guess he thought that I was a nosy neighbor.

"Tiara!!!" Both Karen and Ke-Ke shouted running up to me.

"Excuse me officer," I repeated, trying to get his attention but another officer approached me instead.

"Ma'am who are you, do you own this property?"

"Yes I do," I said.

Karen and Ke-Ke watched me as I spoke to the officer. I could see that they were both crying.

The officer's face was stern. "Ma'am, we are still trying to figure out what went on here, I'm going to need to jot down your information."

A Hood Chick's Story Part II

I was dazed as I watched them carry the young lady's boyfriend from the first floor out on a gurney. He appeared to be in a lot of pain, but I didn't see his girlfriend.

I gave the officer my name and cell phone number but I still didn't have a clue what was going on. Karen and Ke-Ke and I made our way away from that officer and they began explaining but they were both talking fast and shaking.

"Listen, one at a time, what the fuck happened!" I shouted.

"I'm so sorry Tiara, I'm sorry," Ke-Ke cried out.

Karen began speaking as Ke-Ke put her face in her hands crying.

"A'ight T, this is what happened. Last week the first floor chick's boyfriend came up to borrow a DVD so we invited him inside of our apartment. So instead of borrowing the DVD he ended up watching it with us. Ke-Ke also invited Jerry over to chill with her that night. So we were all chilling, watching TV and shit, but when Jerry left, I fell asleep and the dude from the first floor stayed and slept with Ke-Ke."

I looked at Ke-Ke and I was disgusted because I already knew where this conversation was leading.

Karen finished, "So apparently Jerry didn't leave, he sat around in the hallway all night to see when dude from the first floor was leaving our crib. When Ke-Ke walked dude to the door, Jerry was out in the hallway in the cut and when he saw Ke-Ke kissing the dude goodbye, he ran up on him and they started beefing. Shit got real crazy; they broke the hallway lights and put mad holes in the walls."

I was heated. I looked at them both as if they were the same teenage girls getting into the bullshit drama that we got into when we were younger. I had faith in them, I really thought that they had matured and were trustworthy. At this point, they looked completely pitiful to me and I wanted to rip them both a new asshole.

"So there are holes in the walls as of last week and y'all are just now telling me?"

Karen cut me off.

"I'm not done with the story because that was only last week. Jerry didn't only put holes in the hallway either, he did some crazy shit to our apartment that we didn't want to tell you about. But before I get to that, I want to finish telling you what happened tonight."

Ke-Ke was still crying and hadn't taken her head out of her hands. There were several police officers going in and out of the house making out their police report. And I was just pissed off altogether; I didn't know what to do.

Karen finally finished. "Well dude from the first floor's girl works nights so Ke-Ke was with him in his apartment tonight and I guess his girlfriend got off work early and caught him and Ke-Ke in the bed together."

A Hood Chick's Story Part II

I looked into one of the police cars and spotted dude's girlfriend in the backseat staring into space. And then the rest of Karen's story put all the pieces together to the puzzle.

"His girlfriend stabbed him in the arm and him and Ke-Ke came running upstairs to our apartment and that's when I called the police. She didn't run up after them, she was downstairs probably calling you to come out here T. But I'm so sorry; we didn't mean to bring any drama to your house. I had no idea about all this shit, I didn't know Ke-Ke was consistently sleeping with him. It wasn't me that fucked up this time."

Ke-Ke finally lifted her head and put her finger in Karen's face. "Uh-uh bitch! Don't act like you didn't know nothing about this, you didn't have the money to pay Tiara either, you knew exactly what I was doing!" she barked at Karen.

"Hold the fuck up Ke-Ke!" I shouted. "You was fuckin' him for money? Didn't we talk about this shit before! You ain't no different from Renee, what the fuck kind of dumb shit is that? If y'all didn't have the money for the rent, you should have told me, you don't fuck with your neighbor's man, that shit is nasty and it's stupid."

They stood there looking at me like they were two years old. They didn't know what the fuck to say to me and I only had a few words left for them.

205

LaShonda DeVaughn

"Yo, it's a wrap. Ya'll can take your shit and move the fuck out tonight!"

"But T, where are we gonna go?" Karen pleaded.

"That's no longer my problem."

I walked away from them, I couldn't take looking at them, I was fired up.

The police were finally wrapping up. They took my tenant into custody and took her boyfriend to the hospital. I felt so stupid and embarrassed for bringing my girls into this nice neighborhood to have them tearing shit the fuck up. Homeowners were serious about their homes, if you created bad reputations around the neighborhood; it made everyone's property value plummet so I know they were not feeling me at that point.

I went inside of the house and immediately noticed the trail of blood leading from dudes apartment up the stairs from after he got stabbed. The hallway stairs was drenched in blood and the walls had blood smeared fingerprints on them. I opened up Ke-Ke and Karen's apartment and not only was the apartment floors tracked with blood but there was yellow and neon green paint splattered on all of the walls all the way up to the ceiling as well as on all of their furniture. Big ass holes were in the walls as if someone took a sledge hammer and was trying to knock the walls down.

Ke-Ke and Karen walked in behind me a short while later. I stood in the middle of the room looking around at

A Hood Chick's Story Part II

how all my hard work had went down the drain. There was no way that the paint on the shellacked floors and the deep holes in the walls would take just some chump change to fix. I would have to spend all of the money that I saved to fix and clean up the mess that my two "friends" created.

"All of this is what Jerry did to our apartment the day after he had the fight with the dude downstairs. I let him in T, he said he wanted to talk but I didn't know that he was going to go all out and do this," Ke-Ke said pointing to the disaster that her psycho ex Jerry created in their apartment.

I took one last look at the apartment and then at my two whacked out friends and told them for the last time, "Get your shit, and get the fuck off my property." And I left. If I would have stayed a second longer, I would have fought them both but it wasn't even worth it. I knew what I had to do. I had to sell that house and start another plan.

My stable future was once again uncertain.

207

LaShonda DeVaughn

Chapter Fourteen – Super Bowl Sunday

I immediately put the house back on the market. I priced it to sell for as much as I bought it for because I didn't care about getting a profit from it. Instead of the house being something that I was proud of, I now thought of it as a burden because Jerry had fucked it up. Both the first and third floor tenants moved out which meant that I would have to foot the bill for the mortgage on my own and frankly I didn't have the money. I tried not to think too much about my friends because it made me want to go to wherever they were staying and beat the fuck out of both of them. So instead, I tried once again to put some focus on my own family.

I even took myself to the doctor to get a physical. I wanted to be tested for everything, even stress. Doctor Johnson had been my primary care doctor ever since I had Shayonna. She was very approachable and I had taken a liking to her ever since she delivered my baby.

A Hood Chick's Story Part II

She took blood to perform a pregnancy test even though I assured her that I wasn't pregnant. She also performed a pap-smear in which I would have to wait for the results along with the pregnancy test. When she checked my blood pressure she indicated that it was sky high and when I explained to her about some of the problems occurring in my life I hoped that she wouldn't have to prescribe an anti-depressant for me because I was truly a stressed mess and on the verge of depression. Overall, I wanted to see if my health was intact and out of concern my doctor recommended a therapist.

Super Bowl Sunday rolled around and I called myself putting in some work in the kitchen. I made buffalo wings, fried chicken, a special cheesy dip mixed with salsa and cream cheese for the Tortilla chips and splurged on Coronas and Heinekens. Tony and I were on okay terms. He invited a bunch of his niggas over including an overly quiet Shawn. Shawn sat on the couch the whole time while Tony and the rest of his rowdy ass friends cursed the Giants out from taking our history from under our feet. We watched as Tom Brady led the Patriots into a losing battle that would eventually make the moral in Boston low. I don't even think Shawn hit one of the seven blizzes that went around amongst their boys and he was a big smoker like Tony. He didn't even indulge in the fact that the Patriots lost after having a track record of winning every game for the season and would have made history if we would have won the Super Bowl again. Shit I was even mad that the Patriots lost and I don't even watch football like that so I don't know what the fuck Shawn's problem was. He truly was never the same after that shit that went down with Ashley and Takia.

Tony ended up having to fork over three hundred dollars to his boy Cat who happened to be from New York. Cat bet Tony that the Giants would bring it to the Patriots and unfortunately he was right. Cat gracefully took his winnings from Tony and cracked himself another Heineken. That was another thing that pissed me off about Tony, he knew our money situation wasn't right but would still splurge, make bets and other dumb frivolous shit with his money fronting like he was still baller of the year.

I kept my eye on Shawn from the kitchen the entire night because he appeared real strange to me. It was as if he was wearing how he felt on the inside, on the outside. He was frowning for no reason and was completely unfriendly and I wanted his ass out of my house.

All of the noise and commotion from Tony and his friends eventually woke up Shayonna. I heard her small footsteps coming down the stairs and I walked over to the bottom of the staircase. She was rubbing her eyes while walking down and once she saw Shawn, she dashed into the living room and didn't even acknowledge me at the bottom of the stairs.

A Hood Chick's Story Part II

"Hey Uncle Shawn!" She plopped on his lap and gave him a hug.

"Alright Shayonna get off his lap," I said. I didn't play my daughter sitting on no man's lap and she hopped right off. She took Shawn's hand and tugged on it.

"Come upstairs Uncle Shawn, let me show you what my daddy bought me."

Tony smashed the blizz into the ashtray pretending to be jealous, or maybe he was. "Shayonna, you came straight to Shawn and you didn't come and give daddy a kiss."

"Daddy, I already seen you today, I haven't seen Uncle Shawn in a long time." She said extra cheery.

Shawn cracked the first smile since he had been there and Shayonna led him upstairs to show off her new toys.

A half hour passed by and I was in the kitchen cleaning like a slave. I washed the dishes, wiped the countertops and trashed all of the empty bottles that Tony's friends left laying around and needless to say I was tired as shit. Most of his boys had left but a few of them were still in the living room watching the highlights on ESPN and being as loud as they wanted to be.

"Roll up," Tony's cocky ass demanded.

211

LaShonda DeVaughn

Cat sat up off the couch and picked the Dutch master pack off of the coffee table, he cracked it open and prepared it to roll. While doing so Cat glanced up at the ceiling.

"Fuck that nigga Shawn doing playing dress up or some shit?" he asked.

Tony took his foot off the couch and looked up at the ceiling too. "I don't know what the fuck that nigga is up there doing."

He stood to walk to the bottom of the stairs and yelled Shawn's name. "Shawn! What the fuck you up there doing nigga?"

Shawn came walking down the stairs. His face was expressionless.

"Damn nigga, what the fuck was you up there doing, playing dress up, getting your nails painted or some shit?" Tony asked.

"Whatever dog. Yo I'm out."

He walked past Tony and went out the door. Tony watched him as he walked out and went back into the living room with the rest of his boys.

"Yo, this is the last time I'm fuckin with that nigga. He been acting real funny ever since this deal we had went bad. He acts like he can't just charge shit to the game and take a loss like a real nigga would. He's fucking lame that niggas cut." Tony said.

A Hood Chick's Story Part II

"I feel you dog, the nigga was acting real grimy all night." Cat said lighting up the blunt.

"Fuck that nigga," Tony said laying back on the couch.

After cleaning up as much as I could for the night, I decided to go upstairs to run me some bath water. I was exhausted, the balls of my feet were killing me from playing hostess all night and I just wanted to soak my feet and relax. I went into Shayonna's room to check on her when I noticed her lights out, I figured she went back to sleep and proceeded to give her a good night kiss. I placed a peck on her chubby cheek when I noticed that it was moist. As I went to turn on the lights I could hear her whimpering and I quickly flicked on the switch.

"Baby are you crying?"

I sat beside her on her bed, she was balled up lying on her side facing the opposite wall.

"Baby, what's the matter, tell mommy why you're crying?" I asked tugging on her shoulder. When Shayonna didn't answer I pulled her body toward me and I noticed in between her legs were soaked with blood.

I yelled at the top of my lungs for Tony. "Tonyyyyyyy!!!!!!"

Tony zoomed up the stairs when he heard me screaming. He entered the room and then looked at the blood on Shayonna's bed and pajamas.

213

LaShonda DeVaughn

"What the fuck happened?" he screamed out.

"That muthafucka raped our daughter Tony!" I screamed.

Cat ran up the stairs and called the ambulance for us once he saw the blood. We tried to comfort Shayonna, she appeared to be in a lot of pain and we made all of Tony's friends leave the house.

"I'm gonna kill that nigga! I'ma fuckin' murder that bitch ass nigga!" Tony screamed out punching the walls. I sat clutching my daughter and crying. I couldn't even think straight, I just wanted to get her to the hospital.

One good thing about living in the suburbs was that the ambulance arrived about five minutes after Cat called.

We rode inside the ambulance with Shayonna. Tony and I cried like babies all the way to the hospital. It was the most horrible feeling in the world to see our baby in pain when there was nothing we could do about it, it was killing me.

They rushed Shayonna to one of the hospital rooms.

"Sorry, you can't come in here right now, just wait right here, someone will be out to see you," one of the male doctors told us.

Tony and I stood impatiently in the waiting room crying.

Shortly after one of the doctors came out into the hall looking around until she spotted us pacing the hall.

214

A Hood Chick's Story Part II

"Are you Ms. James, Shayonna's mom?"

"Yes I'm Miss James," I said.

"Okay ma'am and is this her father?" she said pointing to Tony.

"Yes," Tony and I said at the same time.

"Okay, why don't you two come over here and have a seat."

At this point I wanted to knock the doctor against the wall for stalling. I just wanted my baby's results, all the small talk was irrelevant. I needed to know NOW.

"Ma'am just tell me what's going on with my daughter!" I said impatiently.

"Well." She paused and then clutched the chart to her chest. "Her insides were bruised pretty badly. There is a lot of scar tissue, however she isn't in too much pain because we have her heavily sedated. Now for the bad news."

"Excuse me? You just told us the bad news," I snapped.

Tony stood up and walked toward me to hold my head while I sat to calm me down.

She continued, "There's a possibility that she may not be able to have children."

"What? What? Hold up, hold up what do you mean!" I shouted. Tears immediately began to flow even harder. I saw tears streaming down Tony's cheeks as well but he tried to hold his composure in order to calm me down.

"Well it looks to me that whoever had done this didn't only force sexual intercourse but there was also some sort of object involved. Now I'm not sure what type of object was used but judging from the scarring and the amount of blood that was lost, we did conclude that a sharp object was used during this assault."

"Tony our baby! Tony she's only five years old!" I cried looking up at him.

He squeezed me tighter and then couldn't fight back his tears. Shayonna was what held us both together and now she was sitting in a hospital bed in unbearable pain. How could I explain to my daughter when she got older that she couldn't bear children because her daddy's friend raped her because he was mad about losing money? This just wasn't fair!

Tony and I both cried as the doctor explained the severity of the situation.

"Usually when there is infertility due to rape, we categorize it as Incidental causes. This category includes damage inflicted on any part of the reproductive system by physical trauma."

She looked at us both like she pitied us. She probably did. I mean we were so young and had no idea how to handle what was going on.

A Hood Chick's Story Part II

"I'm so sorry, I'll come out to get you both when it's an appropriate time to see your daughter. Right now she's highly sedated and I would like for her to get a good amount of undisturbed rest."

The doctor began to walk away and a lady with a stack of papers in her hand came out of a side room passing the doctor and pointing at us. "Are those the parents?"

"Yes," The doctor responded looking back in our direction before leaving the lady standing solo.

The lady proceeded walking toward Tony and me. "Hi, my name is Tonya Lebrowski, I work for DSS," she said.

"DSS?"

"Yes Ma'am, the Department of Social Services."

"I know what DSS stands for, why are y'all getting involved in this?" I spit back.

Tony pat my back to calm me down because getting gully with Social Services wouldn't help matters any.

"Ma'am, anytime something happens to an underage child that endangers their safety while in the care of their guardian, we have to become involved."

"Yes she was under our care, but how were we supposed to know that someone who we let in our home would harm our daughter!" Those last words hurt like a bullet wound. My beautiful daughter was laying in a fuckin' hospital bed drugged up because of that stupid deal with

217

Tony, Shawn and them bitches. And now DSS would be involved in my fuckin' life like I wasn't a good mother, shit was so ugly at that point for me, I was falling apart. All that I could do was look at this stocky lady and try not to cuss her out. She was only doing her job.

"So are you saying that you know who did this to your daughter?" She asked getting her pen ready to write down the suspect's name.

I looked up at Tony. He gave me a look to keep my mouth shut because he wanted to handle Shawn on his own terms.

"No, we don't know who did this, we had a lot of company tonight and we had no idea that someone had went into our daughters room and assaulted her."

She gave me a look as if she knew that I was lying.

"Alright ma'am, I'm sorry for your agony and I do sympathize with you. But more importantly, I sympathize with the child. This is standard procedure, we care about the well-being of the child, she's the real victim here so we have to investigate to see if there is any sign of obvious abuse or neglect from the parents or any other individuals living in the household."

Tony was pissed. Everything started to hit him even harder. The baby, DSS and Shawn's ass. Tony had it in for him. He withdrew his hold from me and rushed out and I knew exactly where he was going but I didn't care at that

A Hood Chick's Story Part II

point. I was too numb to care. Whatever was going to happen to Shawn so be it. All the good in me that I had accumulated over the years died when he touched my daughter. I didn't want to think of what Tony was going to do because there are always repercussions to every action but this situation to me felt different. Anyone who was evil enough to harm a child deserved every bad thing that came their way.

I sat with the stocky lady exchanging information and setting up a time where DSS could come to visit my household to investigate.

The mortgage company was shut down so I had no current paystubs to show her to ensure our lifestyle was legit. I was just all fucked up in the game but right now my main concern was Shayonna.

LaShonda DeVaughn

Chapter Fifteen – Crushed

I allowed Shayonna to rest that night and rushed home to pack some clothes for my hospital stay. My body was so weak, I felt like I hadn't eaten in days. I climbed the stairs, each step harder than the first, until I finally reached the top. My stomach was doing somersaults as I approached my daughter's room. I stepped in and quickly backed into the hallway and stood still against the wall. The sight was too intense for me to stomach. I re-entered her room and tried my hardest not to glance at all of the blood that soaked her twin bed. Over on the floor by her dresser I saw a wire hanger that was twisted and bent. It was covered in blood and seemed to have small pieces of skin tissue hanging from the sharp end. It had to be what Shawn used to take away pieces of my daughter's future.

I vomited all over the floor and ran out of her room. I fell to my knees and cried because I felt violated. This was the beautiful delicate little Angel that God sent for me to protect and I failed. My innocent child was being tormented

220

with a wire hanger and sexually assaulted and I didn't have a clue that it was happening. She didn't deserve this. She didn't deserve to feel a single bit of the strife that I endured my entire life. Why would the world inflict my bad luck on my daughter? It just wasn't fair! I cried and begged God to allow my baby to have a speedy recovery and if any bad thing was aimed her way, I prayed that he would divert it to me instead.

I stood and I screamed.

"Whyyyyy!!!!!" I let out a cry that only someone who had lived a life full of unfulfilled promises and agony could scream out. The type of cries a broken hearted and an unloved soul would scream.

"Whyyyyy!!!!" I let out another long cry as I fell in a squat and rocked my body on the floor. I sat there crying for a good while until my inner strength told me that losing myself wouldn't help Shayonna. I needed to get up and muster some strength to be there for my baby.

I got up and led myself into my bedroom; I stuffed someday clothes and underclothes into my duffle bag. I grabbed my tooth brush as well as a few garments for Tony. I approached my closet to grab a few outfits and sneakers when I noticed that the door to my safe was open. I looked inside and realized that my gun was missing. I searched around hoping that Tony wasn't dumb enough to use my gun to handle Shawn but I didn't have time to dwell on it because my daughter needed me.

I ran out of the house and locked my front door. I noticed a letter sticking out of the mailbox from Trè and I grabbed it and stuffed it into my purse. I flew back up to the hospital and the doctor told me that I still wouldn't be able to see Shayonna for a while. I wanted to cuss her out so badly but I had to maintain a healthy reputation for the sake of DSS.

I didn't know what to do with myself while I sat impatiently in the hospital's small family waiting room alone. I beat myself up about the actions that took place so much that I wanted to harm myself. I realized that I couldn't always depend on myself to handle my grief on my own, I had to reach out to someone, but who could I call? When I discovered that this happened to my baby, all I wanted to do was reach for my own mom to help me with this situation. I wanted to hug her and hear her tell me that everything would be alright. I wanted her to preach to me as she did when I was younger to point out my faults and lead me to the right path. I wanted my mom so badly at that moment that I cried thinking about how much her sensitivity would mean to me at that very moment.

I shut myself into a phone booth in the hospital and searched through the yellow pages for my aunt's phone number. If anyone knew where my mom was, she would.

A Hood Chick's Story Part II

There were about a hundred listings for Brenda James and I called most of them with my cell phone each time coming up short. That's when I spotted Brenda James with an address listed on River Street in Mattapan. I knew that it had to be my aunt because each time she moved, it was always somewhere in Mattapan because it was close to where she worked.

I dialed the number and when the person picked up, I immediately started crying.

It was my mom's voice.

The sound of her voice washed over me and it felt so good.

"Mom." I whispered through my cry.

"Hello, who is this? I can't hear you," she said.

"Mom," I said crying again. I sniffed, "Mom it's me Tiara."

The phone was completely silent.

"Mom I need you right now, you just don't understand how much I really need you right now mom."

I heard my mom let out a silent cry but it seemed as if she was trying to hold it back.

"You don't have to say anything mom, just let me talk. I'm so sorry about Sharod mom, I really am. We all loved him and we all tried to protect him. Please understand mom, it's not me nor Trè's fault that he's gone. We can't control God's plan. Yes I took him out of your household to

223

come live with me in a better neighborhood but I couldn't control what he did when he returned to the hood. I tried to protect him ma, I really did. You can't keep blaming me for what happened because I need you. You don't understand how much I have needed you over the years. I miss you so much mommy it burns my soul. Me and Trè both.

Your granddaughter is five years old now. She's so beautiful mom and she reminds me of Sharod so much." I cried so hard that I had to pause until I caught my breath.

"Right now I'm in the hospital, someone hurt my baby mom, someone took her innocence and I'm hurting so bad right now. I need you to tell me what I'm doing wrong mom, tell me that I'm going to be a good mom and that everything will be okay. You're the only person whose words would mean something to me right now. Mom, my body is worn down, I don't know how much more I could take, I need you mommy." I pleaded like I was six years old again and waited for my mom to make everything okay.

I heard her sniff and each time she tried to talk she kept crying until she was finally gained her composure. "Well Tiara, if it was in God's plans to take Sharod, then it was in his plans for whatever happened to your baby. I lost my baby and now you're feeling the wrath of someone causing pain against yours."

I took the phone away from my ear and just stared at it. All the hope that I had in recovering my relationship with

A Hood Chick's Story Part II

my mom one day was buried into that phone call. It was over, once she hung up in my ear, I realized, I didn't have a mom.

I felt dizzy exiting that phone booth. My legs felt like they were going to give out on me. My heart had been ripped straight out of my body by my mom. I managed to make my way back to the waiting room where I sat feeling puzzled, lonely and weak. My mind was going a million miles a minute. I sat trying to focus on one thing but I couldn't focus at all.

I glanced down at my purse and noticed Trè's letter sticking out. I picked it up and slowly opened it. His letter started out by telling me how much he had missed me and how he hadn't been able to get in contact with me by phone in weeks. All the bullshit with my property, dealing with Tony and my fake ass friends forced me to neglect Trè and I felt horrible about it.

I read on and was crushed even more at his words: *'My appeal was denied'*.

I glanced away from the letter. I didn't know why I had my hopes set on Trè getting out in the first place. To be Tiara James and remain optimistic was a joke because everything always failed for me.

The letter carried good news and bad. The good news was that Trè heard about me going to his block to ask Ken-Ken to get at Tank for Renee. He said that as soon as word got back to him about that, he immediately called it off. He said his niggas wasn't getting into shit over no slut ass bitch. He clarified that whoever got at Tank and shot him was his own enemies and that it had nothing to do with his block. I placed my hand on my chest and took a deep breath because that was such great news to me.

Unfortunately the next paragraph displayed some disturbing news that turned my stomach into knots. He asked me if I had heard about Mumbles and Kal getting killed and asked if I attended their funerals. I couldn't read anymore, I stuffed the letter into my purse and started gagging and then threw up in the empty wastebasket beside me.

Mumbles and Kal, Sharod's homeboys, were killed over something that was most likely senseless and I had no idea about it. I wondered if Turk was with them and how everything went down but I was too sick to keep thinking about it or to read anymore of Trè's letter. That shit hurt me so bad, I couldn't breathe.

"Ms. James, you can come see your daughter now."

The doctor came out to get me and I looked at her like I was a sad sick child. I was a mess and stumbled when I stood. It felt like the world was sitting on my shoulders and that there was nothing I could do to make the weight any lighter. I stopped walking and stood in place to pull myself together. I had to get myself together in case Shayonna was awake. If she was to see me crying, it would only make her feel worse, so I had to be strong.

On my way to the hospital room, I occasionally took deep breaths and shut my eyes thinking about Shayonna and then about Trè's letter. It had to be a sign from God and I got the message loud and clear. It was time to take my daughter and get far, far away from Boston.

When I walked in the hospital room I immediately burst out in tears. My daughter was asleep and the sight of her innocent face tore me apart. The IV's in her arm, the machines, it wasn't fair, it was too much. How could Shawn hurt such an innocent soul? What kind of devil was he?

I brushed my hand over my daughters head staring at her as she slept.

"Mommy's so sorry I couldn't help you baby. Mommy is so sorry. Please forgive me Shayonna, you're all that I have." I cried my heart out.

I kissed her on the cheek and just sat at her bedside staring at her sweet face, appreciating everything about her.

Moments later, she was struggling to open her eyes. They had my baby so drugged up that it was hard for her to stay awake. I quickly wiped my tears so that she wouldn't see them and I smiled to let her know it was okay.

"Hi baby."

"Hi," she whispered as she slipped in and out of consciousness.

227

"How you feeling sweetness?"

"It hurts Mommy." Her eyes rolled back.

It took everything inside of me not to break down. I tucked in both of my lips and bit down hard. Fighting back my tears at that moment was like fighting a war by myself.

She tried to open her eyes again but the medicine was so strong that she fell right back to sleep.

"Just rest beautiful, just rest."

Looking at Shayonna officially confirmed what I needed to do. I was taking my baby girl and getting the fuck away from this madness. I knew that if I stayed in Boston, there would just be something new to hold me back. Even moving into the suburbs didn't keep me away from the hood. There was always some new bullshit that occurred and I wasn't up for anything else, this was my final blow.

Tony rushed into the hospital room about three hours later. I stood up when he walked in but he rushed by me and went straight over to the bed that held Shayonna.

He cried hard. "Baby girl, Daddy's baby, it's gonna be okay." He sniffed rubbing one of her cheeks before turning away. He couldn't keep looking at her on the hospital bed. He started frantically pacing the room like he didn't know what to do next.

It crushed him to see our baby on that gurney just as much as it hurt me. Tony kept crying as we held each other. It was the first time in a long time that we had actually connected. We needed each other at that moment and it felt good to know that we had each other's back. We sat next to Shayonna in the two reclining chairs that the hospital provided.

"T, I did that, I handled that shit," Tony said crying and hugging me.

I knew exactly what he had done but I didn't want to know the details. I had mixed feelings about it. I wanted Shawn hurt very badly for what he did to my daughter; for taking away her future and her innocence. But I didn't think I wanted him dead. That only meant his family would hurt too.

I could tell that Tony felt bad for what he did so I let him continue his confession.

"He's gone T, that motherfucker is gone and he deserved that shit." He pointed to Shayonna. "Look at my fuckin' daughter."

He spilled it all out because it weighed on his conscious. He kept looking at Shayonna and getting sick thinking about what happened to her and then thinking about what he had done to Shawn. After all they did used to be best friends.

"I'm glad I did that shit. You don't hurt my fuckin' daughter, she's my life T, both of y'all man, y'all are my world, I can't believe this shit!" He stood up and went out in the hallway.

LaShonda DeVaughn

I sat impatiently in my chair waiting for him to come back in the room. I had to know how deep my involvement was in what he had done. All I could do was hope that Tony wasn't as stupid as I thought that he was.

He calmed down just enough to come back into the room but he still sat next to me fidgeting, he just couldn't keep still.

I hesitated to ask him at first because I was afraid of his answer. But I had know. "Tony, tell me that you didn't do that using my shit from the safe?" I had to talk in codes just in case people were listening to us in the hospital. He knew that I was asking him if he'd used my gun to kill Shawn.

"T, Shawn kept the two hammers from the time we did that shit at the Holiday Inn so I didn't have a burner."

"Just answer me Tony, does that mean you used mine?"

He turned to look at me and his eyes had already told me the answer. My ass had a license to carry a weapon that now had a body on it.

A Hood Chick's Story Part II

Chapter Sixteen – Recovery

Life went so quickly the next few weeks.

Between DSS visits, being investigated for Shawn's death, and caring for Shayonna, shit was crazy for me. On top of that Tony was still in the game and his responsibilities at home were conveniently put on the backburner.

DSS was making their final visit to my house at six in the damn morning. They had concluded that Shayonna lived in a safe environment and after that day, they didn't have to do any further investigations. Thank God she left the moment she did. As soon as I locked the door dismissing the DSS worker, I went upstairs to prepare some clothes for Shayonna since there was a possibility of her coming home from the hospital that day when all of a sudden, I heard people outside chattering. I ran outside and almost knocked down a frail, well-groomed white man wearing a suit that was standing on my lawn.

"Excuse me, may I help you?"

"Are you the homeowner?" he asked.

"Yes I am, who are you and who are all of these people?" I said gazing out at the crowd of people.

"Ma'am this house is being foreclosed on. We've sent several notices. These people are out here to participate in the auction. We are auctioning off this house to the highest bidder."

"Oh hell no you ain't! You can take your auction and bid on the next person's house." I looked out at everyone. "Y'all can go home now, this house isn't for sale." They all looked at each other confused and the frail man told me that there wasn't anything that I could do about the auction.

Me, with my real estate background knew that there wasn't anything that I could do about the auction but I felt so stupid because I had no idea that Tony wasn't making any of the payments. As soon as I left that responsibility up to him shit went downhill. I don't know why I stayed with his ass so long.

I ran inside.

"Tony! People are outside bidding on the house. You really haven't been paying the mortgage?"

"What Tiara? You're supposed to handle all that shit!" he said bagging up some crack for a play he was about to serve.

"Are you serious Tony? I told you when you said that I just sat around looking pretty that I would no longer be

232

responsible for the bills since that's all you thought of me and I was serious. I can't believe you haven't paid the shit since then Tony, that was months ago!"

"Why the fuck couldn't you do it Tiara? You were paying the bills on your other house."

I was put on the spot, I didn't know that he even knew about my property.

He smirked. "Tiara you really didn't think that Susan would tell me about that? She told me a long time ago when you first started home searching. I was waiting to see when your sneaky ass was going to tell me."

"So what!" I confessed. "That was my responsibility and it's being sold anyway but that's none of your business. I can't believe you wasn't paying the mortgage here Tony, at *our* residence. Were you just waiting for the bank to put us out on the street?"

"Man whatever yo, I'm 'bout to go get this money."

His cocky ass took the drugs off the counter, put his scale away and left to serve his play. He didn't even acknowledge the people auctioning off the house, it was as if he didn't care.

I was pissed at him. The house was in his name and he didn't give a fuck about his credit. However if it was in my name I would have continued to make sure the payments went out on time. But since I wasn't appreciated, I let Tony take over the bills and boy did it bite me in the ass.

LaShonda DeVaughn

I headed up to the hospital to see Shayonna. Tony was also supposed to meet me there after he served his play.

I entered the hospital double doors and I spotted my doctor in the hall.

"Hey Doctor Johnson," I said forcing a smile.

"Oh hey Tiara, I've been trying to get in touch with you. We sent out your results, do you have time to come into my office?"

I looked at her puzzled because I didn't remember receiving anything from the hospital in the mail.

"Well I was just going to see my daughter but okay I'll stop in for a second." I said.

I walked into Doctor Johnson's office praying she wouldn't tell me I was pregnant. I wanted more children but at this particular, unstable point in my life, it would be hard for me to handle the added responsibility.

She sat at the computer and printed out a few sheets first and as they were printing she turned her chair to face me.

"Tiara, your pregnancy test came back negative so you're not pregnant."

I exhaled, that shit was a relief.

"However, you tested positive for gonorrhea. Now I'm going to explain to you what this disease is but in the meantime I'm printing out some literature so that you'll have a better understanding of how it's contracted and maybe you can even share the information with your partner. It is sexually transmitted. And it is very important that we get this cured because the disease can spread to your ovaries and fallopian tubes, resulting in pelvic inflammatory disease."

The room started to spin. I slowly shut my eyes while the doctor continued to explain how the disease is prevented and treated. Tony's cheating had now affected my health and I was finally about to *stop* talking about leaving him and being about it. It scared the shit out of me to think he could have easily infected me with something permanent like Herpes or even worse AIDS.

It could have been Ashley that had infected him or the bitch that left her panties at my house, but whoever the bitch was could have Tony, disease and all, because I was through.

"Here is your prescription and I suggest that you wear condoms from now on." Doctor Johnson handed me the prescription for ceftriaxone and asked if I had any questions.

I shook my head and walked out. I was embarrassed in front of the doctor as if she was one of my friends because that shit tore me up. This nigga really burnt me, the mother of his fuckin' child!

It was curtains for his ass.

I went to see Shayonna and surprisingly Tony was already in there with her.

235

He was smiling and hugging on her and I just wanted to knock him the fuck out. I definitely didn't want to confront him in front of Shayonna, so I was going to have to wait. This was supposed to be a happy day for us since there was a possibility that Shayonna would be discharged, but it was hard to hide my agitation.

"What's wrong Mommy?" Shayonna asked.

I shook my head snapping out of my disgust for Tony.

"Nothing baby. You ready to come home today?"

"Yes Mommy. I feel better, please can I go home today?"

I heard a tap on the door and the doctor entered with a smile. "Yes you are going to be discharged today little missy. No more needles and medicine sweetheart, you can go home with your parents today."

"Yaaay," Shayonna said happily. I knew my baby was tired of the hospital because I was.

I pulled out her jogging suit and laid it beside her.

"Put your clothes on baby."

"Okay mommy."

The doctor directed Tony and me into the hallway to give us Shayonna's status.

"Although Shayonna is being discharged today, I'm afraid that we are still unable to give you good news regarding a fully recovered reproductive system. She is still

A Hood Chick's Story Part II

scarred pretty bad. We are however hoping that things will reverse as she gets older but it's not guaranteed. Only time will tell. The severity of this case was so extreme, we almost had to give her a blood transfusion. But we are glad that she's healed enough to come home and resume being a normal five year old."

"Thank you doctor," I said as she handed us the paperwork.

"You're very welcome," she said before leaving us.

Tony's Aunt approached us as the doctor walked off.

"Are they letting her leave today, can I see her?" she asked. Tony's aunt was in her mid-forty's, she loved Shayonna to death. She spoiled her rotten and didn't mind watching her for us when we needed her. She was the perfect family baby sitter.

"Yes, she's okay, and yes they are letting her leave today," I responded.

Before she went in to see Shayonna I stopped her. "Do you mind if she rides with you back to our house?" I asked.

She smirked. "Now Tiara you know I don't mind. I'm going to take her to get some ice cream first and then we'll be right there."

"Okay perfect, thanks so much."

Tony looked at me. "Why you don't want her to ride back with one of us?"

237

I glared at him like he was the enemy of the state. "Because you need to meet me at the house right now because we need to talk."

"About what? We can talk now."

"Tony, let's be cordial right now and kiss Shayonna goodbye and then meet each other at the crib alright? Trust me, it's important."

Shayonna put on her jogging suit and happily let me know that she was going with her auntie to get some ice cream and I told her that I'd see her when she got home. I hugged and gave her little body a tight squeeze and then headed to the crib.

A Hood Chick's Story Part II

I beat Tony home.

When he got there he immediately started jumping to conclusions. "Yo T, is this about your gun, I tossed that shit in the Charlestown River, I scratched the serial numbers off of it and everything, so trust me, it will never be traced back to you."

"No, it's not about that." I handed him the paperwork from the doctor outlining the STD that he passed on to me.

He read it and then played dumb. "So what the fuck is this?"

"What the fuck do you think it is Tony?"

He shrugged. "What is it?"

"It's the disease you gave me. You been staying out all night claiming to be hustling but you're obviously hustling inside some nasty bitch's pussy. I want to hurt you so bad right now Tony, I can't believe you burnt me."

"Whatever man, I didn't give you that shit!" He threw the papers on the floor.

239

LaShonda DeVaughn

"So who did Tony? I have never cheated on you, *ever*. I stayed faithful through good times and bad. I kept taking you back even after you cheated on me, beat me and disrespected me. I even stayed after finding some bitch's panties in our house. I loved you hard as shit Tony. And I only stayed with you this long because I appreciated you. I still appreciate the shit you did for me. I appreciate you for taking me out of the hood and showing me a life that I probably would have never known.

"But I also held you down when you were in jail. I didn't even look in another man's direction when you were locked up. I devoted myself to my daughter and you and this is how I get paid back? I kept trying to push myself to leave you Tony but it was hard because of how much I love you. And you never appreciated anything that I done for you. I was a rider for you and your business, I loved working with you. And I got repaid by being accused of only sitting around and looking pretty!

"Then when I tried to teach you a lesson and let you handle the bills so that you would see how much you needed me, you let the house go downhill. What else am I supposed to sit around and take from you Tony, huh? And now I find out that you burnt me with gonorrhca and your cocky ass is sitting there not wanting to admit it. I'm done! You'll never change. I've reached the end and I'm not waiting anymore, I'm leaving you now."

A Hood Chick's Story Part II

"Yeah a'ight. You ain't going nowhere. You try to take my daughter out that door, there is going to be problems."

"Tony, save your threats okay. You hit me for the last time once you knocked me out in the bathroom." I shot him a look. "We're done."

I left Tony sitting on the bed and went into the closet and began packing my bags. He eventually got up and went downstairs. I'm not sure if he took me serious but his cocky ass left the room without saying anything.

I was sobbing uncontrollably while stuffing my clothes in my suitcase. It hit me like a ton of bricks that I was actually leaving. This was really it for me. I was leaving the love of my life. I lugged my suitcase into the hallway and set it up against the wall. I started toward Shayonna's room when Tony stormed back up the stairs walking toward me. He pushed me up against the wall and started kissing my neck.

"You ain't leaving me Tiara, I will not let you leave." He sucked on my neck as I tried to push him away.

"Stop Tony, seriously move."

He began feeling on my body grabbing my ass and trying to unbuckle my jeans. He groped on my breast and I pushed his hands away.

"Tony, move!"

LaShonda DeVaughn

"No! You're not leaving me." He wiped the tears from my eyes and looked at me.

"I'm sorry Tiara, I'm sorry for everything okay; we can work this out boo. Please?"

I looked at him and cried harder. "No we can't Tony, not this time."

"Yes we can baby please, Tiara give me another chance," he pleaded.

I tried not to let my soft spot for Tony overcome me and I escaped his grip.

I entered Shayonna's room and quickly stuffed all of her clothes into her suitcase.

Tony stood by the door. "You're serious. You're really taking my daughter and leaving me?"

I didn't answer him. He watched over me as I packed my daughters belongings, her favorite doll and the picture of Sharod that she kept under her pillow. I turned around to carry her suitcase out of her room but he was blocking the door.

"Excuse me Tony."

"You ain't going nowhere." He dropped to his knees and unbuckled my pants trying to eat his way out of this.

"Tony, stop."

I yanked away from him and zipped my jeans back up. He stared in my eyes and read the seriousness of what

242

A Hood Chick's Story Part II

was about to happen. He got up off his knees and just stood there watching me.

Before I could react, he grabbed me by my neck forcing me into the hallway. He grit his teeth talking close to my face. "You are not fuckin' leaving me Tiara." He banged my head up against the wall like three times each bang harder than the other. A tear fell from his eye. "I ain't shit without y'all, I need you T, don't do this to me. I will kill you first. Don't do this Tiara please, I will kill you!" He cried.

I tried to take his arm from my neck but he had put a lot of anger into that hold and I couldn't breathe. He kept squeezing tighter and banging my head against the wall and I was about to past out.

"Daddy what are you doing?" I tried to look over at my daughter at the end of the hallway but Tony's grip on my neck was too tight.

"Tony, get your hands off that girl right now!" his aunt demanded.

Shayonna cried and ran up to me. "Mommy you okay?" I caught my breath and then bent to hug her. "I'm fine baby."

"Daddy why was you hurting mommy?"

Shayonna's face was full of worry. "I'm sorry baby." His voice was barely above a whisper.

I was thankful that I'd left the door unlocked because Tony's aunt was my safe haven to get my suitcases out into my car so that Tony couldn't stop me.

"Tony, don't you ever put your hands on her again," his aunt snapped.

"I'm sorry auntie," Tony said as he watched me rushing the suitcases past him throwing them down the stairs. I only had two suitcases full of clothes and shoes, one for each of us but that was all that we needed. I loaded the suitcases into the car and then came into the house to get my daughter. Tony was standing next to his aunt at the bottom of the stairs holding Shayonna and apologizing to her. For a moment I thought he would put up a fight.

I looked in his eyes, "hand me the baby Tony." I said.

He just looked at me, then at Shayonna and tears fell from his eyes. It hurt me to my soul that I was taking Shayonna away from him but it was for our own good. If I remained with him, he would continue cheating and then eventually he would start to beat me in front of Shayonna and she would end up resenting him like I did my father.

"Give her the baby." Shayonna's aunt said nudging Tony's arm with her elbow. Tony squeezed Shayonna tight and kissed her cheek long and hard before handing her to me. I continued to gaze in his eyes as he passed me Shayonna.

"Thank you," I said to him.

That thank you came from the bottom of my heart. It had more than one meaning. I was thankful to him for saving me from the hood and being there for me. All of our years weren't bad. Anticipating his release from jail was the only thing I'd looked forward to the whole time I lived with Renee in the projects. In a sense, he actually was my knight in shining armor but in reality I had to come to terms with the fact that he wasn't the one. I took his hand and placed my engagement ring inside his palm and walked out the door.

I buckled Shayonna in and backed out of the driveway and looked at our home for the last time before I pulled away.

My heart broke in half and then the tears came. This had to be the same pain my mom felt when she left my father when I was Shayonna's age. I remembered how she kept apologizing to me and my brother Trè.

It was so clear now because I was driving away saying the same thing to Shayonna.

"I'm sorry Shayonna, I'm so sorry."

A Hood Chick's Story Part II

Epilogue

I will always keep in touch with Tony for Shayonna's sake. Although we had our problems, I would never totally cut her out of her father's life. She loved him and he deserved to be in her life, he was always a good father first. But once I get situated in whatever state God brings me to, I wouldn't give him my address; I rather let Shayonna visit him.

I stayed in a hotel the night that I left Tony because I had to be present at the bank for the closing with the new homeowners who bought my three family home off of me. I actually ended up getting a pretty good amount of money from the sale. It was enough to move Shayonna and me away and set us up comfortably until I landed a job in wherever we settled. To be honest, it was enough for me to not work for a year if I wanted to.

Before I left for my journey out of Boston, I went to visit Mumbles and Kal's grief-stricken family's homes to pay my respect for their losses. I wouldn't have felt right leaving if I didn't pay my respects in some way.

A Hood Chick's Story Part II

I went by both of their homes and left the families with envelopes stuffed with a few hundred dollars. Money wouldn't help their pain but it was the least that I could do, especially since I didn't attend either funerals.

Mumbles little cousin was on the porch of his house when I was leaving out and he told me the street they were killed on.

They were killed just a little ways from Mumbles house. I rolled up to put a teddy bear near the pole that everyone used for their memorial and I also lit up one of the candles that were blown out. I took out an old picture of Sharod, Mumbles, Kal and Turk when they were pre-teens chilling in my old spot and I tucked it inside of the teddy bear's snug pocket. I stepped back looking at all of the teddy bears, then I glared at the' we love you' and 'we miss you' signs and I couldn't take anymore.

The sky suddenly turned gray and rain began to fall hard onto the street. I gave my final goodbyes and headed up to Sharod's final resting place to also bid my farewell.

I rode by the hood passing all the old streets that I was finally leaving for good. There were a lot of tears shed and stressful days in my hood that I had to endure that even some men probably wouldn't have been able to handle. As I glanced in the back seat at Shayonna who was looking out of her window, I almost cried at how happy I was that she wouldn't have to know what type of pain these particular streets carried. I had hoped that God put me through everything that I had been through so that Shayonna would ride life's waves effortlessly. These streets took my soul, gave it back and swallowed it again. This time, there would be no way for the streets to defeat me, I was finally leaving.

I realized I couldn't stay in Boston just for Trè anymore either, he was a grown man and I was only one person. As far as keeping money in his canteen, I would always hold him down on that. Other than that, I had to focus on me and Shayonna. I realized that I should have put myself before others a long time ago and I probably wouldn't have went through half of the shit that I had. What was loyalty anyway? Would any of the people that I had ever helped lift a fuckin' finger to help me, hell no! But I always had a fight in me that made me feel as though I was super woman and that I could help everyone. Shit, I couldn't even help myself.

I took out my umbrella to shield us from the rain as Shayonna and I stood in front of Sharod's headstone.

A Hood Chick's Story Part II

I stood there telling Sharod about my plans to leave. It was so painful leaving Boston knowing that his headstone was there and that I wouldn't be able to visit it frequently. But I knew that Sharod would agree to my leaving but it was still so hard. Just as I was about to pour out a stream of tears to contribute to the pouring rain, the rain suddenly stopped but tears were still formed at my eyes. Shayonna pointed toward the sky, "Mommy look, the sun is coming out."

I took down my umbrella, looked up at the sun and it beamed down gracefully over Sharod's headstone.

I smiled and dried my tears and sighed looking at the headstone.

"I got the message loud and clear baby bro. Don't Cry, Just Ride."

I smiled and stared at his headstone for a second. I blew him a kiss, hopped into my car and drove off. I was taking my little brother's advice. He may have never known it when he said it to his old friends but those words were meant for me. Don't Cry Just Ride meant that I would no longer cry for situations that I couldn't control; I had to ride it out and keep it moving because one day it will be okay.

LaShonda DeVaughn

Boston, my engagement to Tony, my mom, my friends, my old life, would merely be memories to me. It felt good letting go of most of my burdens. But there were also some that would stay with me for the rest of my life. The fact that I couldn't recover a relationship with my mom would always haunt me. But as my mom used to always tell me when I was younger, 'Tiara, don't be like me, be better than me' and I plan to do just that. I would never abandon Shayonna. I plan to raise her in a new city and start all over.

And with that being said.

Today will be the beginning of the rest of my life.

I told y'all I wouldn't give up.

Your Girl, Tiara James

A Hood Chick's Story Part II

Acknowledgements

First I would like to thank GOD for the ability to allow me to continue to use my craft to create art. Without him I wouldn't be where I am today. I'm thankful for my two children Shyna and DeVandre, my mom and my two brothers Darryl and Andre.

Dre, little bro, we did it again, I love you and I will continue to keep your memory alive. D, my big bro, hold your head, you'll be home soon enough and I can't wait for your book to drop, the streets are going to go crazy!

To Rahdahl, thanks for continuously believing in me and pushing me to go hard as we made StreetDreamz Publications come into existence; you're greatly appreciated. To every single one of my true friends that had my back throughout my writing career, thank you. Kiyana, Felisha, Precious, Kaie and Nichole, I consider y'all my sisters, thank you for listening to me vent as I grinded. Y'all are the definition of real friends.

I would like to especially thank all of my fans for being patient as Part II was birthed. You guys all

251

hold a special place in my heart and I'm truly thankful for your continued support.

For all the aspiring writers and to all of the young ladies and gentlemen who reach out to me for advice, always remember GRIND TIME EQUALS SHINE TIME. Continue to stay motivated and don't let anyone hold you back from achieving your goals. If I can do it, so can you.

Until we meet again,

LaShonda DeVaughn

Be sure to stop by my website and leave your mark in my guestbook www.Lashondadevaughn.page.tl
Follow me on Twitter @hoodchickstory
Facebook/shondadevaughn
Myspace.com/hoodchick
www.StreetDreamzPublications.com

Be on the lookout for my third novel coming soon titled "If All Men Cheat, All Women Should Too!"

```
Yell  1 800
Chief 1 500
Lum   2400
All   2200
Take  3 000
      8 9 0 0
   1
vet   4 50
Dee   7 00
Mic   3 00
Balli  650
     13 0 0 0
CASH 10 000
TRee  3 000
     28 0 0 0
Balls 4 000
    3 2 0 0 0
Bon   2 500
    3 4 5 0 0
4½    9 0 0 0
   19 3 5 0 0
     37 300
weight 8 1 0 0 0
      8 8 4 00
    8 9 4 0 0
```

LaShonda DeVaughn

2
350
14
1400
150
3900
49

Breinigsville, PA USA
21 September 2010
245701BV00002B/2/P